Rita

Laura Elizabeth Howe Richards

Rita

Copyright © 2024 Bibliotech Press
All rights reserved

The present edition is a reproduction of previous publication of this classic work. Minor typographical errors may have been corrected without note; however, for an authentic reading experience the spelling, punctuation, and capitalization have been retained from the original text.

ISBN: 979-8-88830-909-4

TO

FIVE GIRLS I KNOW

IN THE TOWN OF SAINT JO

If this story should seem extravagant to any of my readers, I can only refer them to some one of the many published accounts of the Spanish-American War. They will find that many delicate and tenderly nurtured girls were forced to endure dangers and privations compared to which Rita's adventures seem like child's play.

L. E. R

CONTENTS

Chapter I	Threatening Weather	1
Chapter II	The Storm Bursts	7
Chapter III	On the Way	12
Chapter IV	The Camp among the Hills	22
Chapter V	To Margaret	33
Chapter VI	In the Night	40
Chapter VII	Camp Scene	48
Chapter VIII	The Pacificos	58
Chapter IX	In Hiding	64
Chapter X	Manuela's Opportunity	74
Chapter XI	Captain Jack	80
Chapter XII	For Life	87
Chapter XIII	Meetings and Greetings	92
Chapter XIV	Another Camp	100
Chapter XV	A Foregone Conclusion	108

CHAPTER I

THREATENING WEATHER

To Señor,

Señor the illustrious Don John Montfort.

Honoured Señor and Brother:—There are several months that I wrote to inform you of the deeply deplored death of my lamented husband, Señor Don Richard Montfort. Your letter of condolation and advice was balm poured upon my bleeding wounds, received before yesterday at the hands of my banker, Don Miguel Pietoso. You are the brother of my adored husband, your words are as if spoken from his casket. You tell me, stay at home, remain in quietness, till these alarms of war are over. Alas! respectable señor, to accomplish this? Havana is since the shocking affair of the Maine in uproar; on each side are threats, are cries, "Death to the Americanos!" My bewept angel, Don Richard, was in his heart Spanish, by birth American; I see brows black upon me—me, a Castilian!—when I go from my house. Already they speak of to burn the houses of wealthy Americans, to drive forth those dwelling in.

Again, señor, my daughter, your niece Margarita—what to do, I ask you, of this young person? She is Cuban, she is fanatic, she is impossible. I apply myself to instruct her as her station and fortune demand, as befits a Spanish lady of rank; she insubordinates me, she makes mockery of my position as head of her house. She teach her parrot to cry "Viva Cuba Libre!" She play at open windows her guitar, songs of Cuban rebels, forbidden by the authorities. I exert my power, I exhort, I command,—she laughs me at the nose, and sings more loud. I attend that in few days we are all the two in prison. What to do? you already know that her betrothed, Señor Santillo de Santayana, is dead a year ago of a calenture. Her grief was excessive; she intended to die, and made preparation costing large sums of money for her obsequies. She forget all now, she says, for her country. In this alarming time, the freedom her father permitted her (his extreme philanthropy overcoming his judgmatism) becomes impossible. I implore you, highly honoured señor and brother, to write your commands to this unhappy child, that she submit herself to me, her guardian in nature, until you can assert your legal potencies. I intend shortly to make retreat in the holy convent of the White Sisters, few miles from here. Rita accompanionates me, and I trust there to change the spirit of rebellion so shocking in a young person unmarried, into the soul docile and sheep-like as becomes a highly native Spanish maiden. The Sisters are of justice celebrated for their pious austerities and the firmness of their rule. Rita will remain with them until peace is assured, or until your emissaries apport distinct advice.

For me, your kind and gracious inquiries would have watered my heart were it not already blasted. Desolation must attend my remaining years; but through them all I shall be, dear señor and brother, your most grateful and in affliction devoted sister and servant,
Maria Concepcion de Naragua Montfort.

Havana, April 30, 1898.

Dearest, dearest Uncle:—My stepmother says she has written to you concerning me. I implore you, as you loved your brother, my sainted father, to believe no single word she says. This woman is of a duplicity, a falseness, impossible for your lofty soul to comprehend. It needs a Cuban, my uncle, to understand a Spaniard. She wants to take me to the convent, to those terrible White Sisters, who will shave my head and lacerate my flesh with heated scourges,—Manuela has told me about them; scourges of iron chains knotted and made hot,—me, a Protestant, daughter of a free American. Uncle John, it is my corpse alone that she will carry there, understand that! Never will I go alive. I have daggers; here on my wall are many of them, beautifully arranged; I polish them

daily, it is my one mournful pleasure; they are sharp as lightning, and their lustre dazzles the eye. I have poison also; a drop, and the daughter of your brother is white and cold at the feet of her murderess. Enough! she will be avenged. Carlos Montfort lives; and you, too, I know it, I feel it, would spring, would leap across the sea to avenge your Rita, who fondly loves you. Hear me swear, my uncle, on my knees; never, never will I go alive to that place of death, the convent. (I pray you to pardon this blot; I spilt the ink, kneeling in passion; what would you have?)
Your unhappy

Rita.

Beloved Marguerite:—I have written to our dear and honoured uncle of the perils which surround me. My life, my reason, are at stake. It may be that I have but a few weeks more to live. Every day, therefore, dearest, let me pour out my soul to you, now my one comfort on earth, since my heart was laid in the grave of my Santayana.

It is night; all the house is wrapped in slumber; I alone wake and weep. I seldom sleep now, save by fitful snatches. I sit as at this moment, by my little table, my taper illuminated, in my peignoir (you would be pleased with my peignoir, my poor Marguerite! it is white mousseline d'Inde, flowing very full from the shoulders, falling in veritable clouds about me, with deep ruffles of Valenciennes and bands of insertion; the ribbons white, of course; maidens should mourn in white, is it not so, Marguerite? no colour has approached me since my bereavement; fortunately black and white are both becoming to me, while that other, Concepcion, looks like a sick orange in either. Even the flowers in my room are solely white.)

It seems a thousand years since I heard from you, my cool snow-pearl of cousins. Write more often to your Rita, she implores you. I pine for news of you, of Uncle John, of all at dear, dear Fernley. Alas! how young I was there! a simple child, sporting among the

Northern daisies. Now, in the whirlwind of my passionate existence, I look back to that peaceful summer. For you, Marguerite, the green oasis, the palm-trees, the crystal spring; for me, the sand storm and the fiery death. No matter! I live and die a daughter of Cuba, the gold star on my brow, the three colours painted on my heart. Good night, beloved! I kiss the happy paper that goes to you. Till to-morrow, and while I live,
Your

Rita.

Havana, May 1, 1898.

Not until afternoon goes the mail steamer, Marguerite, only pearl of my heart. I wrote you a few burning words last night; then I flung myself on my bed, hoping to lose my sorrows for a few minutes in sleep. I slept, a thing hardly known to me at present; it was the sleep of exhaustion, Marguerite. When I woke, Manuela was putting back the curtains to let in the light of dawn. It is still early morning, fresh and dewy, and I am here in the garden. At no time of the day is the garden more beautiful than now, in the purity of the day's birth. I have described it to you at night, with the cocuyos gleaming like lamps in the green dusk of the orange-trees, or the moonlight striking the world to silver. I wish you could see it now—this garden of my soul, so soon, it may be, to be destroyed by ruthless hands of savage Spaniards. The palms stand like stately pillars; till the green plumes wave in the morning breeze, one fancies a temple or cathedral, with aisles of crowned verdure. Behind these stand the banana-trees, rows and rows, with clusters hanging thick, crimson and gold. Would Peggy be happy here, do you think? Poor little Peggy! How often I long to cut down a tree, to send her whole bunches of the fruit she delights in. The mangoes, too! I used to think I could not live without mangoes. When I went to you, it appeared that I must die without my fruits; now their rich pulp dries untasted by my lips: what have I to do with food, save the bare necessary to support what life remains? I am waiting now for my coffee; at this moment Manuela brings it, with the grapefruit and rolls, and places it here on the table of green marble, close by the fountain where I sit. The fountain soothes my suffering heart, as it tinkles in the broad basin of green marble. Nature, Marguerite, speaks to the heart of despair. You have not known despair, my best one; may it be long, long before you do. Among her other vices, this woman, Concepcion, would like to starve me, in my own house. She counts the rolls, she knows how many lumps of sugar I put in my coffee; an hour will dawn—I say no more! I am patient, Marguerite, I am forbearing, a statue, marble in the midst of fire; but beyond a certain point I will not endure persecution, and I say to you, let Concepcion Montfort, the widow of my sainted father, beware!

Adios, my Magnolia Flower! I must feed my birds. Already they are awake and calling the mistress they love. They hang—I have told you—in large airy cages, all round under the eaves of the summer-house beside the fountain. They are beautiful, Margaret, the Java sparrows, the little love-birds, the splendid macaw, the paroquets, and mocking-birds; but king among them all is Chiquito, our parrot, Marguerite, yours and mine, the one link here that binds me to my Northern home; for I may call Fernley my home, Uncle John has said it; the lonely orphan can think of one spot where tender hearts beat for her, not passionately, but with steadfast pulses. Chico is in superb health; he is—I tell you every time—a revelation in the animal kingdom. More than this, he is a bird of heart; he feels for me, feels intensely, in this dark time. Only yesterday he bit old Julio severely; I am persuaded it was his love for me that prompted the act. Julio is a Spaniard of the Spaniards, the slave of Concepcion. He attempted to cajole my Chico, he offered him sugar. To-day he goes with his arm in a sling, and curses the Cuban bird, with threats against his life. Never mind, Marguerite! a time will soon come—I can say no more. I am dumb; the grave is less silent; but do you think your Rita will submit eternally to tyranny and despotism? No, you know she will not, it is not her nature. You look, my best one, for some outbreak of my passionate nature, you attend that the volcano spring some sudden hour into flame, overwhelming all in its path. You are right, heart of my heart. You shall not be disappointed. Rita will prove herself worthy of your love. How? hush! ask not, dream not! trust me and be silent.

Margarita de San Real Montfort.

CHAPTER II

THE STORM BURSTS

Greatly honoured Sir:—I permit myself the privilege of addressing your Excellency, my name being known to you as man of business of late your admired brother, Señor Don Ricardo Montfort. I find myself, señor, in a position of great hardness between the two admirable ladies, Señora Montfort, widow of Don Ricardo, and his beautiful daughter, the Señorita Margarita. These ladies, admirable, as I have said, in beauty, character, and abilities, find it, nevertheless, impossible to live in harmony. As man of affairs, I am present at painful scenes, which wring the heart. Each cries to me to save her from the other. The señora desires to make retreat at the convent of the White Sisters, thrice holy and beatified persons, but of a strictness repugnant to the lively and ardent spirit of the señorita. Last evening took place a terrible enactment, at which I most unluckily assisted. Señora Montfort permitted her lofty spirit to assert itself more strongly than her delicate corporosity was able to endure, and fell into violent hystericality. Her shrieks wanted little of arousing the neighbourhood; the servants became appalled and lost their reason. Señorita Margarita maintained her calmness, and even refused to consider the señora's condition as serious. On the assurance of the young lady and the señora's maid, I was obliged to accept the belief that the señora would shortly recover if left to herself, and came away in deep grief, leaving that illustrious matron—I speak with respect—in fits upon the floor. One would have said, a child of six deprived of its toy. Greatly honoured Señor Montfort, I am a man no longer young. Having myself no conjugal ameliorations, I make no pretence to comprehend the more delicate and complex nature of females. I am cut to the heart; the señora scrupled not to address me as "Old Fool." Heaven is my witness that I have endeavoured of my best lights to smoothen the path for her well-born and at present bereaved feet. But what can I do?

Neither lady will listen to me. The señorita, let me hasten to say, shows me always a tender, I might without too great a presumption say a filial, kindness. I held her in my arms from the day of her birth, señor; she is the flower of the world to me. When she takes me by the hands and says, "Dear old Donito Miguelito, let me do as I desire and all will be well!" I have no strength to resist her. Had I a house of my own, I would take this charming child home with me, to be my daughter while she would; but—a bachelor living in two rooms—what would you, señor? it is not possible. Deign, I beseech you, to consider this my respectful report, and if circumstances are proprietary come to my assistance, or send me instructions how to act.

Accept, señor, the assurance of my perfect consideration, and believe me
Your obedient, humble servant,
Miguel Pietoso.

To the Honourable Señor Don John Montfort.

Honoured and dear Brother:—Since I wrote you last week, things the most frightful have happened. Rita's conduct grew more and more violent and unruled; in despair, I sent for Don Miguel. This old man, though of irreproached character, is of a weakness pitiable to see in one wearing the form of mankind. I called upon him to uphold me, and command Rita to obey the wife of her father. He had only smooth words for each of us, and endeavoured to charm this wretched child, when terror should have been his weapon. I leave you to imagine if she was influenced by his gentle admonitions. To my face she caressed him, and he responded to her caresses. Don Miguel is an old man, eighty years of age, but nevertheless my anger, my just anger, rose to a height beyond my power of control. I fainted from excess of emotion; I lay as one dead, and no heart stirred of my sufferings. Since then I have been in my bed, with no power more than has a babe of the cradle. This morning Margarita came to me and expressed regret for her conduct, saying that she was willing from now to submit herself to my righteous authority. I forgave her,—I am a Christian, dear brother, and cannot forget the principles of my holy religion,—and we embraced with tears. This evening we go to the convent, where I hope to find ease for my soul-wounds and to subdue the frightful disposition of my stepdaughter. I feel it my duty to relate these occurrences to you, dear and honoured brother, for I feel that I may succumb under the weight of my afflictions. We start this evening, and Don Miguel will inform you of our departure and safe arrival at the holy convent, whither he accompanies us.

Permit me to express, dear brother, the sentiments of exalted consideration with which I must ever regard you as next in blood to my adored consort, and believe me
Your devoted,
Maria Concepcion de Naragua Montfort.

Greatly honoured and illustrious Sir:—Let me entreat you to prepare yourself for news of alarming nature. Yesterday evening I was honoured by the commands of the Señora Montfort, that I convey her and Señorita Margarita to the holy convent of the White Sisters. My age, señor, is such that a scene of emotion is infinitely distressing to me, but I could not disobey the commands of this illustrious lady, the widow of my kindest patron and friend. I went, prepared for tears, for outcries, perhaps for violent resistance, for the ardent and high-strung nature of my beloved Señorita Margarita is well known to me. Figure to yourself, honoured señor, my surprise at finding this charming damsel calm, composed, even smiling. She greeted me with her accustomed tenderness; a more enchanting personality does not, I am assured, adorn the earth than that of this lovely child. She bade me have no alarms for her, that all was well, she was reconciled to her lot; indeed, she added that she could not now wish things otherwise. Amazed, but also enchanted with her docility and sweetness, I gave her an old man's blessing, and my prayers that the rigour of the holy Sisters might be softened toward her tender and high-spirited youth. She replied that she had no fear of the Sisters; that in truth she thought they would give her no trouble of any kind. I was ravished with this assurance, having, I may confess it to you, señor, dreaded the contact between the señorita and the holy Mother, a woman of incredible force and piety. But I must hasten my narrative. At seven o'clock last evening two volantes were in readiness at the door of the Montfort mansion. The first was driven by the señora's own man, the second by Pasquale, a negro devoted since childhood to the señorita. The señora would have placed her daughter in the first of these vehicles; but no! the señorita sprang lightly into the second volante, followed by her maid, a young person, also tenderly attached to her. Interposing myself to produce calm, I persuade the admirable señora to take the position that etiquette commanded, in the first carriage. It is done; I seat myself by her side; procession is made. The way to the convent of the White Sisters, señor, is a steep and rugged one; on either hand are savage passes, are mountains of precipitation. To conceive what happened, how is it possible? When we reached the convent gate, the second volante was empty. Assassinated with terror, I make demand of Pasquale; he admits that he may have slept during the long traject up the hill. He swears that he heard no sound, that no word was addressed to him. He calls the saints to witness that he is innocent; the saints make no reply, but that is not uncommon. I search; I rend the air with my cries; alone silence responds to me. The señora is carried fainting into the convent, and I return to Havana, a man distracted. I should say that in the carriage was found the long mantle in which the señorita had been gracefully attired; to its fold a note pinned, addressed me in affectionate terms, begging her dear Donito Miguelito not to have fear, that she was going to Don Carlos, her brother, and all would be well. Since then is two days, señor, that I have not closed the eye. I attend a fit of illness, from grief and anxiousness. In duty I intelligence you of this dolorous event, praying you not to think me guilty of sin without pardon. I have deputed a messenger of trust to scrub thoroughly the country in search of Don Carlos, death to await him if he return without news of my beloved señorita. He is gone now twelve hours. If it arrive me at any moment the tidings, I make instantly to convey them to your Excellency, whether of joy or affliction.

Receive, highly honoured señor, the assurance of my consideration the most elevated.

Miguel Pietoso.

CHAPTER III
ON THE WAY

"Ah, señorita! what will become of us? I can go no farther. Will this wilderness never end?"

"Courage, Manuela! Courage, daughter of Cuba! See, it is growing light already. Look at those streaks of gold in the east. A few moments, and the sky will be bright; then we shall see where we are going, and all will be well. In the meantime, we are free, and on Cuban soil. What can harm us?"

Rita looked around her with kindling eyes. She was standing on a rock that jutted from the hillside; it was a friendly rock, and they had been sleeping under it, wrapped in their warm cloaks, for the night was cool. A group of palms nodded their green plumes over the rock; on every side stretched a tangle of shrubs and tall grasses, broken here and there by palms, or by rocks like this. Standing thus in the early morning light, Rita was a picturesque figure indeed. She was dressed in a blouse and short skirt of black serge, with a white kerchief knotted around her throat, and another twisted carelessly around her broad-brimmed straw hat. Her beautiful face was alight with eager inquiry and determination; her eyes roved over the landscape, as if seeking some familiar figure; but all was strange so far. Manuela, crouching at the foot of the rock, had lost, for the moment, all the fire of her patriotism. She was cold, poor Manuela; also, she had had a heavy bag to carry, and her arms ached, and she was hungry, and, if the truth must be told, rather cross. It was absurd to bring all these things into the desert. What use for the white silk blouse, or the lace fichu? but indeed they had no weight, whereas this monster of a—

"How is Chico?" asked Rita, coming down from the rock. "Poor bird! what does he think of our wandering? he must be in need of food, Manuela. You brought the box of seed?"

12

"I did, señorita; as to the need of birdseed in a wilderness of hideous forest, I have nothing to say. My fingers are so cramped from carrying this detestable cage, I shall never recover the full use of them. But the señorita must be obeyed."

"Assuredly she must be obeyed!" said Rita; and a flash of her eyes added force to the words. "Could I have come away, I ask you, and left this faithful, this patriot bird, to starve, or be murdered outright? Old Julio would have wrung his neck, you know it well, Manuela, the first time he spoke out from his heart, spoke the words of freedom and patriotism that his mistress has taught him. Poor Chiquito! thou lovest me? thou art glad that I brought thee away from that place of tyranny and bloodshed? speak to thy mistress, Chico!"

But Chico's spirits had been ruffled, as well as Manuela's, by being carried about in his cage, at unseemly hours, when he should have been hanging quietly in the verandah, where he belonged. He looked sulky, and only said, "Caramba! no mi gusta!"

"He is hungry! he starves!" cried Rita; "give me the seed!" Sitting down on the rock, she proceeded to feed the parrot, as composedly as if they were indeed on the wide shaded verandah, instead of on a wild hillside, far from sight or sound of anything human.

"And the señorita's own breakfast?" said Manuela at last, when Chiquito had had enough, and had deigned to relax a little, and even to mutter, "Mi gustan todas!" "Is the señorita not also dying of hunger? for myself, I perish, but that is of little consequence, save that my death will leave the señorita alone—with the parrot."

Rita burst into merry laughter. "My poor Manuela!" she said. "Thou shalt not perish. Breakfast? we will have it this moment. Where is the bag?"

The bag being produced,—it really was a heavy one, and it was hardly to be wondered at that Manuela should be a little peevish about it,—Rita drew from it a substantial box of chocolate, and a tin of biscuits. "My child, we breakfast!" she announced. "If kings desire to breakfast more royally, I make them my compliment. For free Cubans, bread and chocolate is a feast. Feast, then, Manuela mine. Eat, and be happy!"

Bread—or rather, delicate biscuits, and chocolate, were indeed a feast to the two hungry girls. They nibbled and crunched, and Manuela's spirits rose with every bite. Rita's had no need to rise. She was having a real adventure; her dreams were coming true; she was a bona-fide heroine, in a bona-fide "situation." "What have we in the bag, best of Manuelas?" she asked. "I told you in a general way; I even added some trifles, for Carlos's comfort; poor dear Carlos! But tell me what you put in, my best one!"

Manuela cast a rueful glance at the plump valise.

"The white silk blouse," she said; "the white peignoir with swansdown."

"In case of sickness!" cried Rita, interrupting. "You would not have me ill, far from my home, and bereft of every slightest comfort, Manuela? surely you would not; I know your kind heart too well. Besides, the peignoir weighs nothing; a feather, a puff of vapour. Go on! what else?"

"Changes of linen, of course," said Manuela. "The gold-mounted toilet-set; two bottles of eau de Cologne; cigarettes for the Señorito Don Carlos; bonbons; the ivory writing-case; the feather fan; three pairs of shoes—"

"Enough! enough!" cried Rita. "We shall do well, Manuela. You have been an angel of thoughtfulness. You did not bring any jewels? no? I thought perhaps the Etruscan gold set, so simple, yet so rich, might suit my altered life well enough; but no matter. After all, what have I to do with jewels now? The next question is, how are we to find Carlos?"

"To find Don Carlos?" echoed Manuela. "You know where he is, señorita?"

"But, assuredly!" said Rita, and she looked about her confidently. "He is—here!"

"Here!" repeated Manuela.

"In the mountains!" said Rita, waving her hand vaguely in the direction of the horizon. "It is a search; we must look for him, without doubt; but he is—here—somewhere. Come, Manuela, do not look so despairing. I tell you, we shall meet friends, it may be at any turn. The mountains are full of the soldiers of Cuba; the first ones we meet will take us to Carlos."

"Yes," said Manuela. "But what if we met the others, señorita? what if we met the Spanish soldiers first? Hark! what was that?"

A sound was heard close behind them; a rustling, sliding sound, as if something or somebody were making his way swiftly through the tall grass. Manuela clutched her mistress's arm, trembling; Rita, rather pale, but composed, looking steadily in the direction of the noise. It came nearer—the grass rustled and shook close beside them; and out from the tufted tangle came—three large land-crabs, scuttling along on their ungainly claws, and evidently in a hurry. Manuela uttered a shriek, but Rita laughed aloud.

"Good luck!" she said. "They are good Cubans, the land-crabs. Many a good meal has Carlos made on them, poor fellow. If we followed them, Manuela? They may be going—somewhere. Let us see!"

The crabs were soon out of sight, but the two girls, taking up their burdens, followed in the direction they had taken, along the hillside, going they knew not whither.

There seemed to be some faint suggestion of a path. The grasses were bent aside, and broken here and there; something had trodden here, whether feet of men or of animals one could not tell. But glad to have any guide, however insufficient, the girls amused themselves by trying to discover fresh marks on tree or shrub or grass-clump. It was a wild tangle, palms and mangoes, coarse grass and savage-looking aloes, with wild vines running riot everywhere. So far, they had seen no sign of human life, and the sun was now well up, his rays beating down bright and hot. Suddenly, coming to a turn on the hillside, they heard voices; a moment later, and they were standing by a human dwelling.

At first sight it looked more like the burrow of some wild animal. It was little more than a hole dug in the side of the clay bank. Some boughs and palm-leaves were wattled together to form a rustic porch, and under this porch three people were sitting, on the bare ground,—two women, one young, the other old, and a little child, evidently belonging to the young woman. They were clothed in a few rags; their cheeks were hollow with famine, their eyes burning with fever. The old woman was stirring a handful of meal into a pot of water; the others looked on with painful eagerness. Rita recoiled with a low cry of terror. She had heard of this; these were some of the unhappy peasants who had been driven from their farms. She had never seen anything like it before. This—this was not the play she had come to see.

The women looked up, and saw the two girls standing near. Instantly they began to cry out, in wailing voices. "Go! go away! there is nothing for you; nothing! we have not more than a mouthful for ourselves. Take yourselves away, and leave us in peace."

Rita came forward, the tears running down her cheeks. "Oh, poor things!" she cried. "Poor souls, I want nothing. I am not hungry! See!—I have brought food for you. Quick, Manuela, the bag—the biscuits, child! Give them to me! Here, thou little one, take this, and eat; there is plenty more!"

The famished child looked from the biscuit to the glowing face that bent over it. It made a feeble movement; then drew back in fear. The old woman still clamoured to the girls to go away; but the younger snatched the biscuit, and began feeding the child hastily, yet carefully. "Mother, be still!" she said, imperiously. "Hush that noise! do you not see this is no poor wretch like ourselves? This is a noble lady come from heaven to bring us help. Thanks, señorita!" With a quick, graceful movement, she lifted the hem of Rita's dress and pressed it to her lips. "We were dying!" she said, simply. "It was the last morsel; we meant to give it to the little one, and some one might find it when we were dead, and keep the life in it."

"But, eat; eat!" cried Rita, filling the hands of both women with chocolate and biscuits. "It is dreadful, terrible! oh, I have heard of it, I have read of it, but I had not seen, I had not known. Oh, if my cousin Margaret were here, she would know what to do! Eat, my poor starving ones. You shall never be hungry again if I can help it."

The child pulled its mother's ragged gown.

"Is it an angel?" it asked, its mouth full of chocolate.

"Hear the innocent!" said the mother. "No, lamb, not yet an angel, only a noble lady on the road to heaven. See, señorita! he was pretty, while his cheeks were round and full. Still, his eyes are pretty, are they not?"

"They are lovely! he is a darling!" cried Rita; and she took the child in her arms, and bent over him to hide the tears. Was this truly Rita Montfort? Yes, the same Rita, only awake now, for the first time now in her pretty idle life. She felt of the little limbs. They were mere skin and bone; no sign of baby chubbiness, no curve or dimple. Indeed, she had come but just in time. "Listen!" she said, presently. "Where do you come from? where is your home?"

The old woman made a gesture as wide and vague as Rita's own of a few minutes before. "Our home, noble lady? the wilderness is our home to-day. Our little farm, our cottage, our patch of cane, all gone, all destroyed. Only the graves of our dead left."

"We come from Velaya," said the young woman. "It is miles from here; we were driven out by the Spaniards. My father was killed before our eyes; she is not herself since, poor soul; do we wonder at it? we have wandered ever since. My husband—do I know if he is alive or dead? He was with our men, he knows nothing of what has happened. If he returns, he will think us all dead. Poor Pedro! These are the conditions of war, señorita."

She spoke very quietly; but her simple words pierced deeper than the plaints of the poor old woman.

"Listen, again!" said Rita. "I am going to my brother; he also is with our army; he is with the General. Do you know, can you tell me, in what direction to look for them? When I find them, I will see; I will have provision made for you. You must stay here now, for a few hours; but have courage, help will come soon. My brother Carlos and the good General will care for you. Only tell me where to find them, and all will be well."

She spoke so confidently that hope and courage seemed to go from her, and creep into the hearts of the forlorn creatures. The baby smiled, and stretched out its little fleshless hands for more of the precious food; even the old grandmother crept a little nearer, to kiss the hand of their benefactress, and call on all the saints to bless her and bring her to Paradise. The younger woman said there had been firing yesterday in that direction, and she pointed westward over the brow of a hill. They had seen no Cuban soldiers since they had been here, but a boy had passed by this morning, on his way to join the General, and he took the same westerly direction, and said the nearest pickets were not far distant.

"And why did you not follow him?" asked Rita. "Why did you not go with him, and throw yourself at the feet of our good General, as I will do for you now? Yes, yes, I know; you were too weak, poor souls; you had no strength to travel farther. But I am young and strong, and so is Manuela; and we will go together, and soon we will come again, or send help for you. Manuela, will you come with me? or will it be better for you to stay and care for these poor ones while I seek Don Carlos?"

But Manuela was, very properly, scandalised at the thought of her young lady's going off alone on any such quest. It appeared, she said, as if the señorita had left her excellent intelligence behind in Havana. These people would do very well now; they had food; they had, indeed, all there was, practically, and the señorita might herself starve, if they did not find Don Carlos soon. That was enough, surely; let them remain as they were.

"You are right, Manuela!" said Rita, nodding sagely. "We must go together. Your heart does not appear to be stirred as mine is; but never mind—the hungry are fed, and that is the thing of importance. Farewell, then, friends! How do they call you, that I may know how to tell those whom I shall send?"

The younger woman was named Dolores, she said. Her husband was Pedro Valdez, and this old one was his mother. If the señorita should see Pedro—if by Heaven's mercy he should be with the General at this moment, all would indeed be well. In any case, their prayers and blessings would go with the señorita and her valued attendant.

Often and often, the soft Spanish speech of compliment and ceremony sounded hollow and artificial in Rita's ears, even though she had been used to it all her life; but there was no doubting the sincerity of these earnest and heartfelt thanks. Her own heart felt very warm, as she turned, with a final wave of the hands, to take a last look at the little group by the earth-hovel.

"We have made a good beginning, Manuela," she said. "We have saved three lives, I truly believe. Now we shall go on with new courage. I feel, Manuela, that I can do anything—meet any foe. Ah! what is that? a snake! a horrible green snake! I faint, Manuela! I die—no, I don't. See, I am the sister of a soldier, and I am not going to die any more, when I see these fearful creatures. Manuela, do you observe? I—am—firm; marble, Manuela, is soft in comparison with me. Ah, he is gone away. This is a world of peril, my poor child. Let us hasten on; Carlos waits for us, though he does not know it."

Talking thus, with much more of the same kind, Rita pushed on, and Manuela followed as best she might. Rita had left the parrot's cage under charge of Dolores, and carried the bird on her shoulder, with only a cord fastened to his leg. Chico was well used to this, and made no effort to fly away; indeed, he had reached an age when it was more comfortable to sit on a soft shoulder and be fed and petted, than to flutter among strange trees and find his living for himself; so he sat still, crooning to himself from time to time, and cocking his bright yellow eye at his mistress, to see what she thought of it all.

It was hard work, pushing through the jungle. The girls' hands were scratched and torn with brambles; Rita's delicate shoes were in a sad condition; her dress began to show more than one jagged rent. Still she made her way forward, with undaunted zeal, cheering the weary Manuela with jest and story. Indeed, the girl seemed thoroughly transformed, and her Northern cousins, who had known and loved her even in her wilful indolence, would hardly have recognised their Rita in this valiant maiden, who made nothing of heat, dust, or even scorpions, and pressed on and on in her quest of her brother.

After an hour of weary walking, the girls came to a road, or something that passed for a road. There was no sign of life on it, but there was something that made them start, then stop and look at each other. Beside the rough path, in a tangle of vines and thorny cactus, stood the ruin of a tiny chapel. A group of noble palms towered above it; from the stony bank behind it bubbled a little fountain. The door of the chapel was gone; it was long since there had been glass in the windows, and the empty spaces showed only emptiness within; yet the bell still hung in the mouldering belfry; the bell-rope trailed above the sunken porch, its whole length twined with flowering creepers. It was a strange sight.

"Manuela!" cried Rita; "do you see?"

"I see the holy chapel," said Manuela, who was a good Catholic.

"Some saintly man lived here in old times. Pity, that the altar is gone. It must have been a pretty chapel, señorita."

"The bell!" cried Rita. "Do you see the bell, Manuela? what if we rang it, to let Carlos know that we are near? It is a good idea, a superb idea!"

"Señorita, I implore you not to touch it! For heaven's sake, señorita! Alas, what have you done?"

Manuela clasped her hands, and fairly wailed in terror, for Rita had grasped the bell-rope, and was pulling it with right good will. Ding! ding! the notes rang out loud and clear. The rock behind caught up the echo, and sent it flying across to the hill beyond. Ding! ding! The parrot screamed, and Rita herself, after sounding two or three peals, dropped the rope, and stood with parted lips and anxious eyes, waiting to see what would come of it.

CHAPTER IV

THE CAMP AMONG THE HILLS

A sound of voices! eager voices of men, calling to one another. The tread of hasty feet, the noise of breaking bushes, of men sliding, jumping, running, hurrying, coming every instant nearer and nearer. What had Rita done, indeed? Manuela crouched on the mouldering floor at her mistress's feet, too terrified even to cry out now; Rita Montfort drew her dagger, and waited.

Next instant the narrow doorway was thronged with men; swarthy black-browed men, ragged, hatless, shoeless, but all armed, all with rifle cocked, all pressing forward with eager, wondering looks.

"Who rang the bell? what has happened?"

A babel of voices arose; Rita could not have made herself heard if she would; and, indeed, for the moment no words came to her lips. But there was one to speak for her. Chiquito, the old gray parrot, raised his head from her shoulder, where he had been quietly dozing, and flapped his wings, and cried aloud:

"Viva Cuba Libre! viva Garcia! viva Gomez! a muerto Espana!" There was a moment's silence; then the voices broke out again in wild cries and cheers.

"Ah, the Cuban bird! the parrot of freedom! Welcome, señorita! You bring us good luck! Welcome to the Cuban ladies and their glorious bird! Viva Cuba Libre! viva Garcia! viva el papageno! long life to the illustrious lady!"

Rita, herself again, stepped from the chapel, erect and joyous, holding the parrot aloft.

"I thank you, brothers!" she said. "I come to seek freedom among you; I am a daughter of Cuba. Does any among you know Don Carlos Montfort?"

The babel rose again. Know Don Carlos? but surely! was he not their captain? Even now he was at the General's quarters, consulting him about the movements of the next day. What joy! what honour for the poor sons of Cuba to form the escort of the peerless sister of Don Carlos to headquarters! But the distance was nothing. They would carry the señorita and her attendant; they would make a throne, and transport them as lightly as if swans drew them. Ah, the fortunate day! the lucky omen of the blessed parrot!

They babbled like children, crowding round Chiquito, extolling his beauty, his wisdom, the miracle of his timely utterance. Chiquito seemed to think, for his part, that he had done enough. He paid no attention to the blandishments of his ragged admirers, but turned himself upside down, always a sign of contempt with him, said "Caramba!" and would say nothing more.

A little procession was formed, the least ragged of the patriots leading the way, Rita and Manuela following. The others crowded together behind, exclaiming, wondering, pleased as children with this wonderful happening. Thus they crossed a ragged hill, threaded a grove of palms, and finally came upon an open space, roughly cleared, in the middle of which stood a tent, with several rude huts around it. The soldiers explained with eager gestures. Behold the tent of the illustrious General. Behold the dwelling of Don Rodrigo, of Don Uberto, of Don Carlos; behold, finally, Don Carlos himself, emerging from the General's tent. The gallant ragamuffins drew back, and became on the instant spectators at a play. A slender young man came out of the tent, evidently to inquire the meaning of the commotion. At what he saw he turned apparently to stone, and stood, cigarette in hand, staring at the vision before him. But for Rita there was no hesitation now. Running to her brother, she threw her arms around his neck with unaffected joy.

"Carlos!" she cried. "I have come to you. I had no one else to go to. They were taking me to the convent, and I would have died sooner. I have come to you, to live or die with you, for our country."

Manuela wept; the soldiers were moved to tears, and brushed their ragged sleeves across their eyes. But Carlos Montfort did not weep.

"Rita!" he said, in English, returning his sister's caress affectionately, but with little demonstration of joy. "What is the meaning of this? what induced you—how could you do such a thing as this? where do you come from? how did you find your way?" And he added to himself, "And what the mischief am I to do with you now you are here?"

Rita explained hastily; gave a dramatic sketch of her adventures, not forgetting the unfortunate peasants, who must, she said, be rescued that instant from their wretched plight; and wound up with a vivid description of the bell-ringing, the gathering of the patriot forces, and the magnificent behaviour of her beloved Chiquito.

"Good gracious! you have brought the parrot, too!" cried poor Carlos. "Rita! Rita! this is too much."

At this moment a new person appeared on the scene. A tall old man, stooping his head, came out from the tent, and greeted the wandering damsel with grave courtesy.

Perhaps the General had seen too much of life and of war to be surprised at anything; perhaps he was sorry for the embarrassment of his young lieutenant, and wished to make things easier for him; however it was, he apparently found it the most natural thing in the world for a young lady and her maid to be wandering in the wilderness in search of the Cuban army. The first thing, he said, was to make the señorita comfortable, as comfortable as their limited powers would allow. She would take his tent, of course; it was her own from that instant; but equally of course neither Rita nor Carlos would hear of this. A friendly dispute ensued; and it was finally decided that Rita and Manuela were to make themselves as comfortable as might be in Carlos's own tent, while he shared that of his commander. The General yielded only under protest to this arrangement; yet he did yield, seeing that resistance would distress both brother and sister. Since the señorita would not take his tent, he said, the next best thing was that she should accept his hospitality, such as he could offer her, within it; or rather, before it, since the evening was warm. His men were even now preparing the evening meal; when the señorita was refreshed and rested, he hoped she and Don Carlos would share it with him.

Rita withdrew into the little hut, in a glow of patriotism and enthusiasm. "Manuela," she cried, "did you ever see such nobleness, such lofty yet gracious courtesy? Ah! I knew he was a man to die for. How happy we are, to be here at last, after dreaming of it so long! I thrill; I burn with sacred fire—what is the matter, Manuela? you look the spirit of gloom. What has happened?"

Manuela was crouching on the bare earthen floor, her shoulders shrugged up to her ears, her dark eyes glancing around the tiny room with every expression of marked disapproval. It was certainly not a luxurious apartment. The low walls were of rough logs, the roof was a ragged piece of very dingy canvas, held in place by stones here and there. In one corner was a pile of dried grass and leaves, with a blanket thrown over it,—evidently Don Carlos's bed. There was a camp-stool, a rude box set on end, that seemed to do duty both for dressing and writing table, since it was littered with papers, shaving materials, cigarette-cases, and a variety of other articles.

Manuela spread out her arms with a despairing gesture. Was this, she asked, the place where the señorita was going to live? Where was she to hang the dresses? where was she to lay out the dressing things? As to making up the bed,—it would be better to die at once, in Manuela's opinion, than to live—Here Manuela stopped suddenly, for she had seen something. Rita, whose back was turned to the doorway of the hut, was rating her severely. Was this Manuela's patriotism, she wished to know? had she not said, over and over again, that she was prepared to shed the last drop of blood for their country, as she herself, Rita, was longing to do? and now, when it was simply a question of a little discomfort, of a few privations shared with their brave defenders, here was Manuela complaining and fretting, like a peevish child. Well! and what was the matter now?

Manuela had risen from her despairing position, and was now bustling about the hut, brushing, smoothing, tidying up, with an air of smiling alacrity. But indeed, yes! she said; the señorita put her to shame. If the señorita could endure these trials, it was not for her poor Manuela to complain. No, indeed, sooner would she die. And after all, the hut was small, but that made things more handy, perhaps. The beautiful table that this would become, if she might remove the Señor Don Carlos's cigar-ashes? There! a scarf thrown over it—ah! What fortune, that she had brought the crimson satin scarf! Behold, an exhibition of beauty! As for the bed, she had heard from—from those who were soldiers themselves, that no couch was so soft, so wooing to sleep, as one of forest boughs. It stood to reason; there was poetry in the thought, as the señorita justly remarked. Now, with a few nails or pegs to hang things on, their little apartment would be complete. Let the señorita of her goodness forget the foolishness of her poor Manuela; she should hear no more of it; that was a promise.

Rita looked in amazement at her follower; the girl's eyes were sparkling, her cheeks flushed, and she could not keep back the smiles that came dimpling and rippling over her pretty face.

"But what has happened to you, Manuela?" cried Rita. "I insist upon knowing. What have you seen?"

What had Manuela seen, to produce such a sudden and amazing change? Nothing, surely; or next to nothing. A ragged soldier had strolled past the door of the hut; a black-browed fellow, with a red handkerchief tied over his head, and a black cigar nearly a foot long; but what should that matter to Manuela?

Rita looked at her curiously, but could get no explanation, save that Manuela had come to her senses, owing to the noble and glorious example set her by her beloved señorita.

"Well!" said Rita, turning away half-petulantly. "Of course I know you are as changeable as a weathercock, Manuela. But as you were saying, if we had a few nails, we should do well enough here. I will go ask the Señor Don Carlos—"

"Pardon, dearest señorita!" cried Manuela, hastily. "But what a pity that would be, to disturb the señor during his arduous labours. Without doubt the illustrious Señor Don Generalissimo (Manuela loved a title, and always made the most of one) requires him every instant, in the affairs of the nation. I—I can find some one who will get nails for us, and drive them also."

"You can find some one?" repeated Rita. "And whom, then, can you find, pray?"

"Only Pepe!" said Manuela, in a small voice.

Was the name a conjuring-spell? It had hardly been spoken when Pepe himself stood in the doorway, ducking respectfully at the señorita, but looking out of the corners of his black eyes at Manuela. Rita smiled in spite of herself. Was this ragamuffin, barefoot, tattered, his hair in elf-locks,—was this the once elegant Pepe, the admired of himself and all the waiting-maids of Havana? He had once been Carlos's servant, when the young Cuban had time and taste for such idle luxuries; now he was his fellow soldier and faithful follower.

"Well, Pepe," said Rita; "you also are here to welcome us, it appears. That is well. If you could find us a few nails, my good Pepe? the Señor Don Carlos is occupied with the General at present, and you can help us, if you will."

Where had Rita learned this new and gracious courtesy? A few months ago, she would have said, "Pepe! drive nails!" and thought no more about it. Indeed, she could have given no explanation, save that "things were different." Perhaps our Rita is growing up, inside as well as outside? Certainly the pretty airs and graces have given way to a womanly and thoughtful look not at all unbecoming to any face, however beautiful.

The thoughtful look deepened into anxiety, as a sudden recollection flashed into her mind. "Oh!" she cried. "And here I sit in peace, and have done nothing about those poor creatures in the hut! I must go to the General! But stay! Pepe, do you know—is there a man in the camp called Pedro Valdez?"

But, yes! Pepe said. Assuredly there was such a man. Did the señorita require him?

"Oh, please bring him!" said Rita. "Tell him that I have something of importance to tell him. Quick, my good Pepe!"

Pepe vanished, and soon returned, dragging by the collar a lean scarecrow even more dilapidated than himself. Apparently the poor fellow had been asleep, and had been roughly clutched and hauled across the camp, for his hair was full of leaves and grass, and he was rubbing his eyes and swearing softly under his breath, vowing vengeance on his captor.

"Silence, animal!" said Pepe, admonishing him by a kick of the presence of ladies; "Behold the illustrious señorita, who does you the honour to look at you. Attention, Swine of the Antilles!"

Thus adjured, poor Pedro straightened himself, made the best bow he could, and stood sheepishly before Rita, trying furtively to brush a few of the sticks and straws off his ragged clothing.

"You are Pedro Valdez?" asked Rita.

At the service of the illustrious señorita. Yes, he was Pedro Valdez; in no condition to appear in such company, but nevertheless her slave and her beast of burden.

"Oh, listen!" cried Rita, her eyes softening with compassion and anxiety. "You have a wife, Pedro Valdez,—a wife and a dear little child, is it not so? and your mother—she is old and weak. When have you seen them all, Valdez? Where did you leave them?"

The man looked bewildered. "Leave them, señorita? I left them at home, in our village. They were well, all was well, when I came away. Has anything befallen them?"

"They are safe! All is well with them now, or will be well, when you go to them. They are near here, Valdez. The Spaniards broke up the village, do you see? Dolores and your mother fled with the little one. The village was burned, and many souls perished; but Dolores was so strong, so brave, that she got the old mother away alive and safe, and the child as well. They have suffered terribly, my poor man; you must look to find them pale and thin, but they are alive, and all will be well when once they have found you."

Seeing Valdez overcome for the moment, Rita hastened to the General's tent and told her story, begging that the husband and father might be allowed to go at once to the relief of his suffering family.

"And he shall bring them here, shall he not?" she cried, eagerly. "They cannot be separated again, can they, dear Señor General? you will make room for Dolores—that is the wife; oh, such a brave woman! and the old mother, and the dear little child!"

The General looked puzzled; a look half quizzical, half sad, stole over his fine face; while he hesitated, Carlos broke out hastily: "Rita! you are too unreasonable! Do you think we are in a city here? do you think the General has everything at his command, to maintain an establishment of women and children? It is not to be thought of. We have no room, no supplies, no conveniences of any kind; they must go elsewhere."

"They can have my house!" cried Rita, "Your house, brother Carlos, which you have given to me. I will sleep in a hammock, under a tree. What matter? I will live on bread and water; I will—"

"My dear young lady!" said the General, interrupting her eager speech with a lifted hand. "My dear child, if an old man may call you so, if only we had bread for all, there would be no further question. We would gladly take these poor people, and hundreds of other suffering ones who fill the hills and valleys of our unhappy country. But—Carlos is right, alas! that I must say it. Here in the mountain camp, it is impossible for us to harbour refugees, unless for a night or so, while other provision is making. Let Valdez bring his family here for the night—we can make shift to feed and shelter them so long. After that—"

He shook his head sadly. Rita clasped her hands in distress. To be brought face to face with the impossible was a new experience to the spoiled child. There was a moment's silence. Then:

"Señor General," she cried, "I know! I see! all may yet be managed. They shall go to our house."

"To—"

"To our house, Carlos's and mine, in Havana. There are servants, troops of them; there is food, drink, everything, in abundance, in wicked, shameful abundance. Julio shall take care of them; Julio shall treat them as his mother and his sister. I will write commands to him; this instant I will write."

Snatching a sheet of paper from the table, she wrote furiously for a moment, then handed the paper to the General with a look of satisfaction. The General—oh, how slow he was!—adjusted his glasses, and read the paper carefully; looked at Rita; looked at Carlos, and read the paper again. Rita clenched her little hands, but was calm as marble, as she assured herself. "Have I the señorita's permission to read this aloud?" asked the old man at last. "It may be that Don Carlos's advice—a thousand thanks, señorita." He read:

"Julio:—The bearer of this is the wife of Pedro Valdez. You are to take her and her family in, and give them the best the house contains; the best, do you hear? put them in the marble guest-chamber, and place the house at their disposal. Send for Doctor Blanco to attend them; let Teresa wait upon them, and let her furnish them with clothes from my wardrobe. If you do not do all this, Julio, I will have you killed; so fail not as you value your life.

"Margarita de San Real Montfort.

"P.S. The Señor Don Carlos is here with me, and echoes what I say. We are with the brave General Sevillo, and if you dare to disobey, terrible revenge will be taken."

"The ardent patriotism of the señorita," said the General, cautiously, "is beautiful and inspiring; nevertheless, is it not possible that a more conciliatory tone might—I would not presume to dictate, but—"

"Oh, Rita!" cried Carlos. "Child, when will you learn that we are no longer acting plays at home? This is absurd!"

With an impatient movement that might have been Rita's own, he snatched the paper and tore it in two. "The General cannot be troubled with such folly!" he said, shortly. "Go to your room, my sister, and repose yourself after your fatigues."

"By no means!" cried the kindly General, seeing Rita's eyes fill with tears of anger and mortification. "The señorita has promised to make my tea for me this evening. Give orders, I pray you, Don Carlos, that Valdez bring his family to us for the night; the rest can well wait for to-morrow's light. The señorita is exhausted, I fear, with her manifold fatigues, and she must have no more anxieties to-day. Behold the tea at this moment! Señorita Rita, this will be the pleasantest meal I have had since I left my home, two years ago."

No anger could stand against the General's smile. In a moment Rita was smiling herself, though the tears still stood in her dark eyes, and one great drop even rolled down her cheek, to the General's great distress. Carlos, seeing with contrition his sister's effort at self-control, bent to kiss her cheek and murmur a few affectionate words. Soon they were all seated around the little table, Rita and the General on camp-stools, Carlos on a box. The tea was smoking hot; what did it matter that the nose of the teapot was broken? Rita had never tasted anything so delicious as that cup of hot tea, without milk, and with a morsel of sugar-cane for sweetening. The camp fare, biscuits soaked in water and fried in bacon fat, was better, she declared, than any food she had ever tasted in her life. To her delight, a small box of chocolate still remained in her long-suffering bag; this she presented to the General with her prettiest courtesy, and he vowed he was not worthy to taste such delicacies from such a hand. So, with interchange of compliments, and with a real friendliness that was far better, the little feast went on gaily; and when, late in the evening, Rita withdrew to her tent, she told Manuela that she had never enjoyed anything so much in her life; never!

CHAPTER V

TO MARGARET

Camp of the Sons of Cuba,

May the —, Midnight.

My Marguerite:—What will you say when your eyes, those calm gray eyes, rest upon the above heading? Will they open wider, I ask myself? Will the breath come quicker between those cool rose-leaves of your lips? "It is true!" you will murmur to yourself. "She has done as she said, as she swore she would. My Rita, my wild pomegranate flower, has kept her vow; she is in the mountains with Carlos; she has taken her place beside the defenders of her country."

Ah! you thought it was play, Marguerite, confess it! You thought the wild Cuban girl was uttering empty breath of nothingness; you have had no real anxiety, you never dreamed that I should really find myself—where now I am. Where is it? Listen, Marguerite! My house—once Carlos's house, now mine by his brotherly gift—stands in a little glen of the hills. An open space, once dry grass, now bare earth, baked by the sun, trodden by many feet; a cluster of palms, a mountain spring gushing from a rock hard by; on every side hills, the brown, rugged hills of Cuba, fairer to me than cloudy Alps of Italy, or those other great mountains of which never can I remember the barbarous names. To teach me geography, Marguerite, you never could succeed, you will remember; more than our poor Peggy history. Poor little Peggy! I could wish she were here with me; it would be the greatest pleasure of her life. For you, Marguerite, the scene is too wild, too stern; but Peggy has a martial spirit under her somewhat clumsy exterior. But I wander, and Peggy is without doubt sleeping at this moment under the stern eye of her schoolmistress. I began to tell you about my house, Marguerite. So small a house you saw never. Standing, I reach up my hand and touch the roof, of brown canvas, less fresh than once it was. Sitting, I stretch out my arms—here is one wall; there—almost, but a few feet between—is the other. In a corner my bed—ah, Marguerite! on your white couch there, with snowy draperies falling softly about you, consider my bed! a pile of dried grasses and leaves, shaken and tossed anew every morning, covered with a camp blanket. I tell you, the gods might sleep on it, and ask no better. In another corner sleeps Manuela, my faithful maid, my humble friend, the companion of my wanderings. Some day you shall see Manuela; she is an excellent creature. Cultivated, no; intellinctual—what is that for a word, Marguerite? Ah! when will you learn Spanish, that I may pour my soul with freedom?—no; but a heart of gold, a spirit of fire and crystal. She keeps my hut neat, she arranges my toilet,—singular toilets, my dear, yet not wholly unbecoming, I almost fancy,—she helps me in a thousand ways. She has a little love-affair, that is a keen interest to me; Pepe, formerly the servant of Carlos, adores her, and she casts tender eyes upon the young soldier. For me, as you know, Marguerite, these things are for ever past, buried in the grave of my hero, in the stately tomb that hides the ashes of the Santillos. I take a sorrowful pleasure in watching the budding happiness of these young creatures. More of this another time.

I sit, Marguerite, in the doorway of my little house. It is the middle hour of the night, when tomb-yards gape, as your Shakespeare says. Am I sleepy? No! The camp slumbers, but I—I am awake, and I watch. I had a very long siesta, too. The moon is full, and the little glade is bathed in silver light. Here in Cuba, Marguerite, the moon is other than with you in the north. You call her pale moon, gentle moon, I know not what. Here she shines fiercely, with passion, with palpitations of fiery silver. The palms, the aloes, the tangled woods about the camp, are black as night; all else is a flood of airy silver. I float, I swim in this flood, entranced, enraptured. I ask myself, have I lived till now? is not this the first real thrill of life I have ever experienced? I alone wake, as I said; the others slumber profoundly. The General in his tent; ah, that you could know him, Marguerite!

that you and my uncle could embrace this noble, this godlike figure! He is no longer young, the snows of seventy winters have blanched his clustering locks; it is the only sign of age. For the rest, erect, vigorous, a knight, a paladin, a—in effect, a son of Cuba. The younger officers regard him as a divinity; they live or die at his command. They are three, these officers; Carlos is one; the others, Don Alonzo Ximenes, Don Uberto Cortez. Don Alonzo is not interesting; he is fat, and rather stupid, but most good-natured. Don Uberto is Carlos's friend, a noble young captain, much admired formerly in Havana. I have danced with him, my cousin, in halls of rose-wreathed marble; we meet here in the wilderness, I with my shattered affections, he with his country's name written on his soul. It is affecting; it is heart-stirring, Marguerite; yet think nothing of it; romance is dead for Margarita Montfort. Carlos is my kind brother, as ever. He was vexed at first at my coming here. Heavens! what was I to do? My stepmother was dragging me to a convent; my days would have been spent there, and in a short time my life would have gone out like a flame. "Out, short candle!" You see I remember your Shakespeare readings, my dearest. Can I forget anything that recalls you to me, half of my heart? If there had been time, indeed, I might have written to my uncle; I might even have come to you; but the hour descended like a thunderbolt; I fled, Manuela with me. The manner of my flight? you will ask. Marguerite, it was managed—I do not boast, I am the soul of humility, you know it!—the manner of it was perfect. Listen, and you shall hear all. You remember that in my last letter—written, alas! in my beloved garden, which I may never see more—I spoke with a certain restraint, even an approach to mystery. It was thus. At first, when that woman proposed to take me to the convent, I was a creature distracted. The fire of madness burned in my veins, and I could think of nothing save death or revenge. But with time came reflection; came wisdom, Marguerite, and inflexible resolve. To those she loves, Margarita Montfort is wax, silk, down, anything the most soft and yielding that can be figured. To her enemies, steel and adamant are her composition. I had two friends in that house of Spaniards; one was Pasquale, good, faithful Pasquale, an under gardener and helper; the other, Manuela, my maid. I have described her to you—enough! I realised that action must be of swiftness, the lightning flash, the volcano fire that I predicted. Do not say that I did not warn you, Marguerite; knowing me, you must have expected from my last letter what must come. I called Manuela to my room, I made pretence that she should arrange my hair. My hair has grown three inches, Marguerite, since I left you; it now veritably touches the floor as I sit. Our holy religion tells us that it is a woman's crown, yet how heavy a one at times! I closed the door, I locked it; I caused to draw down the heavy Persians. Then, tiger-like, I sprang upon my attendant, and laid my hand on her mouth. "Hush!" I tell her. "Not a word, not a sound! dare but breathe, and you may be my death. My life, I tell you, hangs by a thread. Hush! be silent, and tell me all. Tell me who assists Geronimo in the stables since Pablo is ill." Manuela struggles, she releases herself to reply—

"Pasquale!"

It is the answer from heaven. Pasquale, I have said, is my one friend beside Manuela. I say to her, "Do thus, and thus! give these orders to Pasquale; tell him that it imports of your life and mine, saying nothing of his own; that if I am not obeyed, the evil eye will be the least of his punishments, and death without the sacraments the end for him."

Manuela hears; she trembles; she flies to execute my commands. Then, Marguerite—then, what does the daughter of Cuba do? She goes to the wall, to the trophy I have described to you so often. She selects her weapons. Ah, if you could see them! First, a long slender dagger, the steel exquisitely inlaid with gold, in a sheath of green enamel; a dagger for a prince, Marguerite, for your Lancelot or Tristram! Another, short and keen, the blade plain but deadly, cased in wrought leather of Cordova. Last, my machete, my pearl of destructiveness. It was his, my Santayana's; he procured it from Toledo, from the master sword-maker of the universe. The blade is so fine, the eye refuses to tell where it melts into the air; a touch, and the hardest substance is divided exactly in two pieces. The handle, gold, set with an ancestral emerald, which for centuries has brought victory in the field to the arm of the hero who wore it; the sheath—I forget myself; this weapon has no sheath. When a Santillo de Santayana rides into battle, he has no thought to sheathe his sword. These, Marguerite, are my armament; these, and a tiny gold-mounted revolver, a gem, a toy, but a toy of deadly purpose. Enough! I lay them apart, ready for the night. I go to my stepmother, I smile, I make submission. I will do all she wishes; I am a child; her age impresses me with the truth that I should not set my will against hers. Concepcion is thirty on her next birthday; she tells the world that she is twenty, but I know! it grinds her bones when I remind her of her years, as they were revealed to me by a member of her family. So! She is pleased, we embrace, the volantes are commanded, all goes smoothly. I demand permission to take my parrot to the convent; it is, to my surprise, accorded; I know she thought those savage sisters would kill him the first time he uttered his noble and inspiring words.

The night comes, the hour of the departure. To accompany us goes my good Don Miguel, the dear old man of whom I have told you, whom I revere as my grandfather. My heart yearns to tell him all, to cast myself on his venerable bosom and cry, "Come with me; take me yourself to my brother; share with us the perils and glories of the tented field!" But no! he is old, this dear friend; his hair is the snow, his step is feeble. Hardships such as Rita must now endure would end his feeble life. I speak no word; a marble smile is all I wear, though my heart is rent with anguish. The carriages are at the door. Concepcion would have me ride in the first, that she may have her eyes on me at each instant. She suspects nothing, no; it is merely the base and suspicious nature which reveals itself at every occasion. I refuse, I prodigate expressions of my humility, of my determination to take the second place, leaving the first to her; briefly, I take the second volante, Manuela springing to my side. After some discontent, appeased by dear Don Miguel, who is veritably an angel, and wants but death to transport him among the saints, Concepcion mounts in the first volante. I have seen that Pasquale is on the box of mine; I possess my soul, I lean back and count the beats of my fevered pulse, as we ascend the steep road, winding among hills and forests. The convent is at the top of a long, long hill, very steep and rugged; the horses pant and strain; humanity demands that they slacken their pace, that the carriages are slowly, slowly, drawn up the rugged track. The night descends, I have told you, swiftly in our southern climate; already it is dark. On either side of the road are tall shrouded forms, which Manuela takes for sentinels, for Spanish soldiers drawn up to watch, perhaps to arrest us. I laugh; I see they are the aloes only, planted here in rows along the road. Presently, at a turn of the road, a light! a fire burning by the roadside, and soldiers running, real ones this time, to the horses' heads. "Alerta! quien va?" It is the Spanish challenge, Marguerite; it is a piquette of the Gringos, of the hated Spaniards. They peer into the carriages, faces of savages, of brutes, devils; I feel their glances like poisoned arrows. They demand, Don Miguel makes answer, shows his papers. Of the instant these slaves are cringing, are bowing to the earth. "Pass, most honourable and illustrious Señor Don Miguel Pietoso, with the heavenly ladies under your charge!" It is over. The volantes roll on. I clasp Manuela in my arms and whisper, "We are free!" We mingle our tears of rapture, but for a moment only. We approach the steepest pitch of the long hill (it is veritably a mountain), a place beyond conception rugged and difficult. The horses strain and tug; they are at point of exhaustion. I look at Pasquale; Pasquale has served me since my cradle. Does his head move, a very little, the least imaginable motion? It is too dark to see; the moon is not yet risen. But I feel the horses checked, I feel the carriage pause, an instant, a breath only. I step noiselessly to the ground; the volante is low, permitting this without danger. Manuela follows. There is not a sound, not a creak, not the rustle of a fold. Again it is over. The volante rolls on. Manuela and I are alone, are free in the mountains of Cuba Libre.

I have but one thought: my country, my brother! Behold me here, in the society of one, prepared to shed my blood for the other. You would never guess who else is with us; Chiquito, our poor old friend the parrot, the sacred legacy of that white saint, our departed aunt. Could I leave him behind, to unfriendly, perhaps murderous, hands? Old Julio is a Spaniard at heart; Chiquito is a Cuban bird; his very soul—do you doubt that a bird has a soul, when I tell you that I have seen it in his eyes, Marguerite?—his very soul speaks for his country. If you could hear him cry, "Viva Cuba Libre!" The camp is on fire when they hear him. Ah, they are such brave fellows, our soldiers! poor, in rags, half-fed—it matters not! each one is a hero, and all are my brothers. Marguerite, sleep hangs at last upon me. Good-night, beloved; good-night, cool white soul of ivory and silver. I love thee always devotedly. Have no fear for me. It is true that the Spaniards are all about us in these mountains, that at any moment we may be attacked. What of that? If the daughter of Cuba dies by her brother's side, in her country's cause, my Marguerite will know that it is well with her. You will shed a tear over the lonely grave among the Cuban hills; but you will plant a wreath for Rita, a wreath of mingled laurel and immortelle, and it will bloom eternally.

Ever, and with a thousand greetings to my honoured and admired uncle, your

Margarita de San Real Montfort.

CHAPTER VI
IN THE NIGHT

Rita drew a long breath as she folded her letter. She was in a fine glow of mingled affection and patriotic fervour; it had been a great relief to pour it all out in Margaret's sympathetic ear, though that ear were a thousand miles away. Now she really must go to bed. It was one o'clock, her watch told her. It seemed wicked, profane, to sleep under such moonlight as this; but still, the body must be preserved.

"But first," she said to herself, "I must have a drop of water; writing so long has made me thirsty."

She took up the earthen water-jar, but found it empty. Pepe had for once been faithless; indeed, neither he nor Manuela had escaped the witchery of the full moon, and she had had little good of them that whole evening. She glanced at the corner where Manuela lay; the light, regular breathing told that the girl was sound asleep. It would be a pity to wake her from her first sweet sleep, poor Manuela. A year, perhaps a month ago, Rita would not have hesitated an instant; but now she murmured, "Sleep, little one! I myself will fetch the water."

She stepped out into the moonlight, with the jar in her hand. All was still as sleep itself. No sound or motion from huts or tent. Under the palms lay a number of brown bundles, motionless. Dry leaves, piled together for burning? no! soldiers of Cuba, wrapped in such covering as they could find, taking their rest. Alone, beside a little heap of twigs that still smouldered, the sentry sat; his back was turned to her. Should she speak to him, and ask him to go to the spring for her? No; how much more interesting to go herself! Everything looked so different in this magic light; it was a whole new world, the moon's fairyland; who knew what wonderful sights might meet her eyes? Besides, her old nurse used to say that water drawn from a pure spring under the full moon produced a matchless purity of the complexion. Her complexion was well enough, perhaps, but still—and anyhow, it would be an adventure, however small a one.

The girl's feet, in their soft leather slippers, made no sound on the bare earth. The sentry did not turn his head. Silent as a cloud, she stole across the little glade, and passed under the trees at the farther end. Here the ground broke off suddenly in a rocky pitch, down which one scrambled to another valley or glen lying some hundred feet lower; the cliff (for it was steep enough to merit that name) was mostly bare rock, but here and there a little earth had caught and lodged, and a few seeds had dropped, and a tuft of grass or a little tree had sprung up, defying the gulf below. A few feet only from the upper level, just below a group of palms that nodded over the brink, the stream gushed out from the face of the rock, clear and cold. The soldiers had hollowed a little trough to receive the trickling stream, and one had only to hold one's pitcher under this spout for a few minutes, to have it filled with delicious water. Rita had often come hither in the daytime, during the week that had now passed since her arrival at the mountain camp. It was a wild and picturesque scene at any time, but now the effect of the intense white light, falling on splintered rock, hanging tree, and glancing stream was magical indeed. Rita lay down on her face at the edge of the precipice, as she had seen the soldiers do, and lowered her jar carefully. As the water gurgled placidly into the jar, her eyes roved here and there, taking in every detail of the marvellous scene before her. Never, she thought, had she seen anything so beautiful, so unearthly in its loveliness. Peace! silver peace, and silence, the silence of—hark! what was that?

A crack, as of a twig breaking; a rustling, far below in the gorge; a shuffling sound, as of soft shod feet pressing the soft earth. Rita crouched flat to the ground, and, leaning over as far as she dared, peered over the precipice. The bottom of the gorge was filled with a mass of tall grasses and feathery blossoming shrubs, with here and there a tree rising tall and straight. The leaves were black as jet in the strong light. Gazing intently, she saw the branches tremble, wave, separate; and against the dark leaves shone a gleam of metal, that moved, and came nearer. Another and yet another; and now she could see the dark faces, and the moon shone on the barrels of the carbines, and made them glitter like silver.

Swiftly and noiselessly the girl drew back from the brink, crouching in the grass till she reached the shadow of the grove. Then she rose to her feet, still holding her jar of water carefully,—for there was no need of wasting that,—and ran for her life.

A whispered word to the sentry, who sprang quickly enough from his reverie beside the fire; then to the General's tent, then to Carlos, with the same whispered message. "The Gringos are here! Wake, for the love of Heaven!"

In another moment the little glade was alive with dusky figures, springing from their beds of moss and leaves, snatching their arms, fumbling for cartridges. The General was already among them. Carlos and the other officers came running, buckling their sword-belts, rubbing their eyes.

"Where are they?" all were asking in excited whispers. "Who saw them? Is it another nightmare of Pepe's?"

"No! no!" murmured Rita. "I saw them, I tell you! I saw their faces in the moonlight. I went to get some water. They are climbing up the cliff. I did not stop to count, but there must be many of them, from the sound of their feet. Oh, make haste, make haste!"

The General gave his orders in a low, emphatic tone. Twenty men, with Carlos at their head, glided like shadows across the glade, and disappeared among the trees. Rita's breath came quick, and she prepared to follow; but the old General laid a kind hand on her arm. "No, my child!" he said. "You have done your country a great service this night. Do not imperil your life needlessly. Go rather to your room, and pray for your brother and for us all."

But prayer was far from Rita's thoughts at that moment. "Dear General," she implored, with clasped hands, the tears starting to her eyes, "Let me go! let me go! I implore you! I will pray afterward, I truly will. I will pray while I am fighting, if you will only let me go. See! I have come all this way to fight for my country; and must I stay away from the first battle? Look, dear Señor General! Look at my machete! Isn't it beautiful? it is the sword of a hero; I must use it for him. Let me go!" The beautiful face, upturned in the moonlight, the dark eyes shining through their tears, might have softened a harder heart than that of General Sevillo. He opened his lips to reply, his fatherly hand still on her arm, when suddenly a sharp report was heard. A single shot, then a volley, the shots rattling out, struck back and forth from cliff to cliff, multiplying in hideous echoes. Then broke out cries and groans; the crash of heavy bodies falling back among the trees below, and shouts of "Viva Cuba;" and still the shots rang out, and still the echoes cracked and snapped. Rita turned pale as death, and clasped her hands on her bosom. "Ah! Dios!" she cried. "I had forgotten; there will be blood!" and rushing into her hut, she flung herself face downward on her leafy bed.

The perplexed General looked after her for a moment, pulling his grizzled moustache. "Caramba!" he muttered. "To understand these feminines? Decidedly, this charming child must be sent into safety to-morrow." And shaking his head and shrugging his shoulders, he strode in the direction of the firing.

Ten minutes' sharp fighting, and the skirmish was over. The Spanish "guerilla" was scattered, many of the guerilleros lying dead or wounded at the foot of the precipice, the others scrambling and tumbling down as best they might. Carlos and his men had so greatly the advantage in position, if not in numbers, that not a single Cuban was killed, though two or three were more or less seriously wounded. Among these was the unfortunate Pedro Valdez, who had only that evening returned to camp, having left his child and his old mother in a place of safety. His wife had been allowed to remain for a short time in camp, at the request of the surgeon, as she had had some experience in nursing. Now he was shot in the arm, and his comrades lifted him gently, and carried him back. His wife was waiting for him. She seemed to have expected something of the kind, for she made no outcry; she followed quietly to the clump of trees distant a little way from the rest of the camp, where good Doctor Ferrando had the solitary rancho, the case of surgical instruments and the few rolls of bandages that constituted his field hospital. A rough table had been knocked together for operations; otherwise the sick and wounded fared much as the rest did, sleeping on beds of leaves and dry grass, and fighting the mosquitoes as best they might. Here the bearers laid Pedro down, and Dolores took her place quietly at his side, fanning away the insects that hovered in clouds about the wounded man, holding the poor arm while the doctor dressed it, and behaving as if her life had been spent in a hospital.

Doctor Ferrando spoke a few words of approval, but the woman heeded them little; it was a matter of course that where there was suffering, she should be at work. So, when Pedro presently dropped off to sleep, she moved softly about among the wounded men, smoothing a blanket here, changing a ligature there, doing all with light, swift fingers whose touch healed instead of hurting.

She was sitting beside a lad, the last to be brought in from the scene of the skirmish, when the screen of bushes by the rancho was parted, and Rita appeared. Slowly and timidly she drew near; her face was like marble; her eyes looked unnaturally large and dark. Dolores made a motion to rise, but a gesture bade her keep her place.

"Hush!" said the young girl. "Sit still, Dolores! I have come—to—to learn!"

"To learn, señorita?" repeated the woman, humbly. The señorita was in her grateful eyes a heaven-descended being, whose every look and word must be law; this new bearing amazed and puzzled her.

"What can this poor soul teach the noble and high-born lady?" she asked, sadly. "I know nothing, not even to read; I am a poor woman merely. The señor doctor is this moment gone to take his distinguished siesta; do I call him for the señorita?"

Rita shook her head, and crept nearer, gazing with wide eyes of fear at the prostrate form beside which Dolores was sitting.

"See, Dolores!" she said; and her tone was as humble as the woman's own. "I must learn—to take care of him—of them!" She nodded at the sufferer. "All my life, you see, I could never bear the sight of blood. To cut my finger, I fainted at the instant. Always they said, 'Poor child! it is her delicacy, her sensibility;' they praised me; I thought it a fine thing, to faint, to turn pale at the word even. Now—oh, Dolores, do you see? I desire to help my country, my brother, all the heroes who are risking their life, are shedding their—their blood—for Cuba. I think I can fight; I forget; I see only the bright shining blades, the victorious banners; I forget that these heroes must bleed, that this horrible blood must flow in streams, in torrents, that oceans of it must overwhelm us, the defenders of my country. Ay de mi! I begged the General even now to let me fight, to let me stand beside my Carlos, and wield my beautiful machete. Suddenly, Dolores—I heard the shots; I heard—terrible sounds! screams—oh, Dios!—screams of men, perhaps of my own brother, in anguish. All at once it came over me—I cannot tell you—I saw it all, the blood, the wounds, the horror to death. I awoke from my dreams; I was a child, do you see, Dolores? I was a child, playing at war, and thinking—thinking the thoughts of a silly, silly child. Now I am awake; now I know—what—what war means. So—I am foolish, but I can learn; I think I can learn. You are a brave woman; I have been watching you through the leaves for half an hour. I saw you—I saw you change those cloths; those terrible bloody cloths on that poor man's head. At first my eyes turned round, I saw black only; but I opened them again, I fixed them on what you held, I watched. Now I can bear quite well to look at it. Help me, Dolores! teach me—to help as you help; teach me to care for these brothers, as you do."

Dolores looked earnestly in the beautiful young face. In spite of the deadly pallor, she saw that the girl was fully herself, was calm and determined. With a simple, noble gesture she lifted Rita's slender hand to her lips, saying merely: "This hand shall bring blessing to many! come, my señorita, and see! it is so easy, when once one knows the way of it."

Very gently the poor peasant's wife showed the rich man's daughter the A B C of woman's work among the sick and suffering. At first Rita could do little more than control her own nerves, and fight down the faintness that came creeping over her at sight of the bandaged faces, ghastly under the brown, of the torn flesh and nerveless limbs. Gradually, however, she began to gain strength. The rough brown hand moved so easily, so lightly; it laid hold of those terrible bandages as if they were mere ordinary bits of linen. Surely now, she, Rita, could do that too. As Dolores took a cloth from her husband's head, the girl's hand was outstretched, took it quietly, and handed a fresh one to the nurse. The cloth she took was covered with red stains. For a moment Rita's head swam, and the world seemed to turn dark before her eyes; but she held the thing firmly, till her sight cleared again; then dropped it in the tub of water that stood ready, and taking up the fan of green palm-leaf, swept it steadily to and fro, driving the clouds of flies and mosquitoes away from the sufferer.

Coming back from his siesta half an hour later, good Doctor Ferrando paused a moment at the entrance of the hospital grove. There were two nurses now; the good man gazed in astonishment at the slender figure kneeling beside one of the rough cots, fanning the wounded man, and singing in a low, sweet voice, a song of Cuba. Several of the men were awake, and gazing at her with delight. Dolores, with a look of quiet happiness on her face, sat beside the bed where her husband was sleeping peacefully. "Come!" said the doctor, "war, after all, has its beauty as well as its terror. Observe this heavenly sight, you benevolent saints!" he waved his cigar upward, inviting the attention of all attendant spirits. "Consider this lovely child, awakened to the holiness of womanhood! and the General will destroy all this to-morrow, from respect for worldly conventions! He is without doubt right; yet, what a pity!"

CHAPTER VII

CAMP SCENE

"If I must, dear Señor General—I will be good, I will, indeed; but my heart will break to leave Carlos, and the camp, and you, Señor General."

"My dear child,—my dear young lady, what pleasure for me to keep you here! the first sunshine of the war, it came with you, Señorita Margarita. Nevertheless, duty is duty; I should be wanting in mine, most wofully and wickedly wanting, if I allowed you to remain here, in hourly danger, when a few hours could place you in comparative safety. Perfect safety, I do not promise. Where shall we find it, even for our nearest and dearest, in this poor distracted country? But with Don Annunzio and his family you will be safe at least for a time; whereas here—" The General looked around, and shrugged his shoulders, spreading his hands out with a dramatic gesture. "The Gringos have learned the way to our mountain camp; they will not forget it. Another attack may come any night; our camp is an outpost, placed of purpose to guard this position, which must of necessity be one of danger. To have women with us—it is not only exposing them to the terrible possibilities of war, but—"

He paused. "I see!" cried Rita. "I see! you are too kind to say it, but we are a burden upon you. We make harder the work; we are an encumbrance. Dear Señor General, I go! I fly! Give me half, a quarter of an hour, and I am gone. Never, never, will I be in the way of my country's defenders; never! Too long we have stayed already; Manuela shall make on the instant our packets, and in a little hour you shall forget that we were here at all."

The good General cried out, "No! no! my dear child, my dear señorita; cease these words, I implore you. You cut me to the heart. Consider the help that you have brought to us; consider the nursing, the tender care that you and the wife of Valdez have given to our sufferers, in the rancho there. Never will this be forgotten, rest assured of that. But—it is true that you must go; yet not too soon. This evening, when the coolness falls, Don Carlos, with a chosen escort, will conduct you to the residence of Don Annunzio. There, I rejoice to think that you will find, not luxury, but at least some few of the comforts of ordinary life. Here you have suffered; your lofty spirit will not confess it, but you have—you must have suffered, delicate and fragile as you are, in the rough life of a Cuban camp. Enough! The day is before you, dearest señorita. I pray you, while it lasts, make use of me, of all that the camp contains, in whatever way you can imagine. I would make the day a pleasant one, if I might. Command me, dear señorita, in anything and everything. The camp is yours, with all it contains."

He bowed with courtly grace, and Rita courtsied and then turned quickly away, to hide the tears that would come in spite of her. It was a keen disappointment. When Carlos told her that morning that she must leave the camp, she had refused pointblank. A stormy scene followed, in which the old Rita was only too much in evidence. She raged, she wept, she stamped her little foot. She was a Cuban, as much as he was; she was a nurse, a daughter of the army; no human power should drive her from the ground where she was prepared to shed her last drop of blood for the defenders of her country. Now—a few kind, grave words from a gray-haired man, and all was changed. She was not a necessity, she was a hindrance; she saw that this must be so; the pain was sharp, but she would not show it; she would never again lose her self-control, never. Carlos should see that she was no longer a child. He had called her a child, not half an hour ago, a naughty child, who was making trouble for everybody. Well—Rita stood still; the thought came over her suddenly,—it was true! she had been childish, had been naughty. Suppose Margaret or Peggy should behave so, stamping and storming; how would it seem? Oh, well, that was different. Their blood was cool, almost cold. It flowed sluggishly in their veins. She was a child of the South; it was not to be expected that she should be like Margaret. Yes! but—the thought would come, troubling all her mind; suppose Margaret were here, with her calm sense, her cheerful face, and tranquil voice; would not she be of more use, of more help, than a girl who could not help screaming when she was in a passion?

These thoughts were new to Rita Montfort. Full of them, she walked slowly to her hut, with bent head, and eyes full of unshed tears. Meanwhile, the good General went back to his tent, where Carlos awaited him with some anxiety.

"Well?" he asked, as the gray head bent under the tent-flaps.

"Well," responded his commander. "It is very well, my son. The señorita—she is adorable, do you know it? Never have I seen a more lovely young person! The señorita is most reasonable. She comprehends; she understands the desolation that it is to me to send away so delightful a visitor; nevertheless—she accepts all, with her own exquisite grace."

Carlos shrugged his shoulders; that same exquisite grace had flashed a dagger in his eyes not ten minutes before, vowing that it should be sheathed in the owner's heart before she left the camp; but it was not necessary to say this to the General. Carlos was an affectionate brother, and was honestly relieved and glad to find that Rita had come to her senses. He thanked General Sevillo warmly for his good offices, and, being off duty, went in search of his sister, determining that he would make her last day in camp a pleasant one, so far as lay in his power. He found Rita sitting sadly in the door of her hut, watching Manuela, who was packing up their belongings, unwillingly enough. Manuela had enjoyed her stay in camp greatly, and thought life would be very dull, in comparison, at Don Annunzio's cottage; but there was no escape, and the white silk blouse and the swansdown wrapper went into the bag with all the other fineries.

"Come, Rita," said Carlos, taking his sister's hand affectionately; "come with me, and let me show you some things that you have not yet seen. You must not forget the camp. Who knows? Some day you may come back to pay us a visit."

Rita shook her head, and the tears came to her eyes again; but she drove them back bravely, and smiled, and laid her hand in her brother's; and they passed out together among the palm-trees.

Manuela looked after them, and laid her hand on her heart; it was a gesture that she had often seen her mistress use, and it seemed to her infinitely touching and beautiful. "Ohimé," sighed Manuela. "War is terrible, indeed! To think that we must go away, just when we are so comfortable. But where, then, is this idiot? Pepe! When I call you, will you come, animal? Pepe!"

The thicket near the rancho rustled and shook, and Pepe appeared. This young man presented a different figure from the forlorn one that had greeted the two girls on their first arrival at the camp. His curly hair was now carefully brushed and oiled. The scarlet handkerchief was still tied about his head, but it was tied now with a grace that might have done credit to the most dandified matador in the Havana ring. His jacket was neatly mended; altogether, Pepe was once more a self-respecting, even a self-admiring youth. Also, he admired Manuela immensely, and lost no opportunity of telling that she was the light of his eyes and the flower of his soul. He was now beginning some remarks of this description, but Manuela interrupted him, laying her pretty brown hand unceremoniously on his lips.

"For once, Pepe, endeavour to possess a small portion of sense," she said. "Listen to me! We must leave the camp."

"How then, marrow of my bones! Leave the camp? You and I?"

"I am speaking to a monkey, then, instead of a man? The use, I ask you, of addressing intelligent remarks to such a corporosity? My mistress and I, simpleton. This General of yours drives us from his quarters; he begrudges the morsel we eat, the rude hut that shelters us. Enough! we go; even now I make preparation. Pull this strap for me, Pepe; at least you have strength. Ah! If I were but a great stupid man, it would be well with me this day!"

"But well for no one else, my idol," said Pepe, tugging away at the strap. "Desolation and despair for the rest of mankind, Rose of the Antilles. Accidental death to this bag! why have you filled it so full? There! it is strapped. Manuela, is it possible that I live without you? No! I shall fall an easy victim to the first fever that comes; already I feel it scorching my—"

"Oh, a paralysis upon you! Can I exercise my thoughts, with the chatter of a parrot in my ears? Attend, then, Pepe,—you will miss me a little, will you? Just a very little?"

Pepe opened his mouth for new and fiery protestations, but was bidden peremptorily to shut it again.

"I desire now to hear myself speak," said Manuela. "I weary, Pepe, for the sound of my own poor little voice. Listen, then! These days I have been here, and you have never asked me what I brought with me for you; brought all that cruel way from the city. I knew I should find you somewhere, my good Pepe; or, if not you, some other friend, some other good son of Cuba. I thought of you, I remembered you, even in the rush of our departure. See! It is yours. May it bring you fortune!"

She handed him a little packet, neatly folded in white paper, and tied with a crimson ribbon. Receiving it with dramatic eagerness, Pepe opened it and looked with delight at its contents.

"A detente!" he cried. "Manuela! and the most beautiful that has been seen upon the earth. This is not for me! No! Impossible! The General alone is worthy to wear this object of an elegance so resplendent."

Reassured on this point, he proceeded to pin the emblem on his jacket, and contemplated it with delighted pride. It was a simple thing enough; a square of white flannel the size of an ordinary needlebook, neatly scalloped around the edge with white silk. In the centre was embroidered a crimson heart, and under it the words, "Detente! pienso en ti!" ("Be of good cheer! I think of thee!")

"And did you really think of me, Manuela?" cried the delighted Pepe. "Did you, bright and gay, in the splendid city, think of the lonely soldier?"

"Yes, I did," said Manuela, "when I had nothing else to do. And now you may go away, Pepe, I am busy; I cannot attend to you any longer."

"But," said Pepe, bewildered, "you called me, Manuela."

"Yes; to strap my bag. It is done; I thank you. It is finished."

"And—you have given me the detente, moon of my soul!"

"Then you cannot complain that I never gave you anything. And now I give you one thing more,—leave to depart. Adios, Don Pepe!" and she actually shut the door of the hut in the face of her astonished adorer, who departed muttering strange things concerning the changeableness of all women, and of Manuela in particular.

Meanwhile, Rita and Carlos were wandering about the camp, and Rita was seeing, as her brother promised, some things that were new to her, even after a stay of nearly a week. She saw the kitchen, or what passed for a kitchen,—a pleasant spot under a palm-tree, where the cook was even then toasting long strips of meat over the parilla, a kind of gridiron, made by simply driving four stakes, and laying bits of wood across and across them, then lighting a fire beneath.

"But why does it not burn up, your parilla?" asked Rita of the long, lean, coffee-coloured soldier, picturesque and ragged, who was turning the strips with a forked stick.

"Pardon, gracious señorita, it does burn up; not the first time, nor perhaps the second, but without doubt the third."

"And then?"

"And then,—it is but to build another. An affair of a moment, señorita."

"But does not the meat often fall into the fire when it breaks?"

"Sufficiently often, most noble. What of that? It imparts a flavour of its own; one brushes off the ashes—soldiers do not dine at the Hotel Royal, one must observe. May I offer the señorita a bit of this excellent beef? This has not fallen down at all, or at most but once, one little time."

Rita thanked him, but was not hungry. At least she would have a cup of guarapo, the hospitable cook begged; and he hastened to bring her a cup of polished cocoanut shell, filled with the favourite drink, which was simply hot water with sugar dissolved in it. Rita took the cup graciously, and drank to the health of the camp, and to the freedom of Cuba; the cook responded with many bows and profuse thanks for the honour she had done him, and the brother and sister passed on.

"There are some good bananas near here," said Carlos; "little red ones, the kind you like, Rita. I'll fill a basket for you to take with you; Don Annunzio's may not be so good."

They were making their way through a tangle of tall grass and young palm-trees, when suddenly Rita stopped, and laid her hand on her brother's arm.

"Look!" she said. "Look yonder, Carlos! The grass moves."

"A snake, perhaps," said Carlos; "or a land-crab. Stand here a moment, and I will go forward and see."

He advanced, looking keenly at the clump of yellowish grass that

Rita had pointed out. Certainly, the grass did move. It quivered, waved from side to side, then seemed to settle down, as if an invisible hand were pulling it from below. Carlos drew his machete, and bent forward; whereupon a loud yell was heard, and the clump of grass shot up into the air, revealing a black face, and a pair of rolling eyes.

"What is it?" cried Rita, in terror. "Carlos, come back to me! It is a devil!"

"Only a scout!" said her brother, laughing. "One of our own men on outpost duty. Have peace, Pablo! your hour is not yet come."

"Caramba! I thought it was, my captain!" said the negro scout, grinning. "Better be a crab than a Cuban in these days."

He was a singular figure indeed. From head to waist he was literally clothed in grass, bunches of it being tied over his head and round his neck and shoulders, falling to his thighs. A pair of ragged trousers of no particular colour completed his costume. A more perfect disguise could not be imagined; indeed, except when he lifted his head, he was not to be distinguished from the clumps and tufts of dry grass all about him.

"Pablo is a good scout!" said Carlos, approvingly. "No Gringo could possibly see you till he stepped on you, Pablo; and then—"

"And then!" said Pablo, grinning from ear to ear; and he drew his machete and went through an expressive pantomime which, if carried out, would certainly have left very little of Gringo or any one else.

"Is your post near here? show it! The señorita would like to see how a Cuban scout lives."

Pablo, a man of few words, gave a pleased nod, and scuttled away through the bush, beckoning them to follow. Rita, stepping carefully along, holding her brother's hand, kept her eyes on the scout for a few moments; then he seemed to melt into the rest of the grass, and was gone. A few steps more, and they almost fell over him, as his black face popped up again, shaking back its grassy fringes.

"Behold the domicile of Pablo!" he said, with a magnificent gesture. "The property, with all it contains, of the señorita and the Señor Captain Don Carlos."

Brother and sister tried to look becomingly impressed as they surveyed the domain. Close under a waving palm-tree a rag of brown canvas was stretched on two sticks laid across upright branches stuck in the ground. Under this awning was space for a man to sit, or even to lie down, if he did not mind his feet being in the sun. A small iron pot, hung on three sticks over some blackened stones, showed where the householder did his cooking; a heap of leaves and grass answered for bed and pillows; this was the domicile of Pablo.

Breaking a twig from a neighbouring shrub, the scout bent over the pot, and speared a plantain, which he offered to Rita with grave courtesy. She took it with equal dignity, thanking him with her most gracious smile, and ate it daintily, praising its flavour and the perfection of its cooking till the good negro's face shone with pleasure.

"And you stay here alone, Pablo?" she asked. "How long? you are not afraid? No, of course not that; you are a soldier. But lonely! is it not very lonely here, at night above all?"

Pablo spread out his hands. "Señorita, possibly—if it were not for the crabs. These good souls—they have the disposition of a Christian!—sit with me, in the intervals of their occupations, and are excellent company. They cannot talk, but that suits me very well. Then, there is always the chance of some one coming by—as to-day, when the Blessed Virgin sends the señorita and the Señor Don Carlos. Also at any moment the devil may send me a Gringo; their scouts are as plenty as scorpions. No, señorita, I am not lonely. It is a fine life! In a prison, you see, it would be quite otherwise."

"But there are other ways of living, Pablo, beside scouting and going to prison," said Rita, much amused.

"Without doubt! Without doubt!" said Pablo, cheerfully. "And assuredly neither would befit the señorita. May she live as happy as she is beautiful, the sun being black beside her. Adios, señorita; adios, Señor Captain Don Carlos!"

"Adios, good Pablo! good luck to you and your crabs!" and laughing and waving a salute, they left the scout nodding his grass-crowned head like a transformed mandarin, and went back to the camp.

CHAPTER VIII

THE PACIFICOS

A long, low adobe house, brilliantly white with plaster; a verandah with swinging hammocks; the inevitable green blinds; the inevitable cane and banana patch; this was Don Annunzio's. Don Annunzio Carreno himself (to give him his full name for once, though he seldom heard or used it) sat in a large rocking-chair on the verandah, smoking. He was enormously stout and supremely placid, and he looked the picture of peace and prosperity, in his spotless white suit and broad-brimmed hat.

To Rita, weary after her ten miles' ride from the camp, the whole place seemed a page out of a picture-book. Her mind was filled with rugged and startling images: the rude hospital, with its ghastly sights and homely though devoted tendance; the ragged soldiers, with head or arm bound in bloody bandages; the camp fire and kitchen, the scout in his grassy panoply. Her eyes had grown accustomed to sights like these, and the bright whiteness of house and householder, the trim array of flower-beds and kitchen-garden, struck her as strange and artificial. She felt as if Don Annunzio ought to be wound up from behind, and was whimsically surprised to see him rise and come forward to meet them.

Carlos made his explanation, and presented General Sevillo's letter. Don Annunzio's hat was already in his hand and he was bowing to Rita with all the grace his size allowed; but now he implored them to enter the house, which he declared he occupied henceforward only at their pleasure.

"If the señorita will graciously descend!" said the good man. "On the instant I call my wife. Prudencia! Where are you, then? Visitors, Prudencia; visitors of distinction. Hasten quickly!"

A woman appeared in the doorway; tall and lean, clad in brown calico, with a sun-bonnet to match, but with apron and kerchief as snowy as Don Annunzio's "ducks."

"For the land's sake!" said Señora Carreno.

Rita looked up quickly.

"Visitors, my love!" Don Annunzio explained rapidly, in good enough English. "The Señor Captain and the Señorita Montfort, bringing a note from his Excellency General Sevillo. The señorita will remain with us for some days; I have placed all at her disposal; I—"

"There, Noonsey!" said the lady, not unkindly. "You set down, and let me see what's goin' on."

She laid a powerful hand on her husband's shoulder, and pushed him into his chair again; then advanced to the verandah steps, regarding the newcomers with frank but cheerful scrutiny.

"What's all this?" she said. "Good mornin'! Yes, it's a fine day. Won't you step in?"

Carlos told his story, and asked permission for his sister and her maid to spend some days at the house until some permanent place could be found for her.

The señora considered with frowning brows, not of anger but of consideration.

"Well," she said, "I did say I wouldn't take no more boarders. I had trouble with the last ones, and said I'd got through accommodatin' folks. Still—I dunno but we could manage—does she understand when she's spoke to—English, I mean?"

"Yes, indeed, I do!" cried Rita, coming forward. "I am only half Cuban; it is good to hear you speak. If you will let me stay, I will try to give little trouble. May I stay, please?"

"Well, I guess you may!" cried the New England woman. "You walk right in and lay off your things, and make yourself to home. The idea! Why didn't you say—why, it's as good as a meal o' victuals to hear you speak. Been to the States, have you? Well, now, if that don't beat all! Noonsey, you go and tell José we shall want them chickens for supper. Set down, young man! This your hired gal, dear? Does she speak English? Well no, I s'pose not."

She said a few words to Manuela in Spanish which, if not melodious, was intelligible, and then led Rita into the house, talking all the way.

"Here's the settin'-room; and here's the spare-room off'n it. There! lay your things on the bed, dear. I keep on talkin', when all the time I want to hear you talk. It is good to hear your native speech, say what they will. Husband, he does his best, to please me; but it's like as though he was speakin' molasses, some way. Been in the States to school, did you say?"

Rita told her story: of her American father, who had always spoken English with her and her brother; of the summer spent in the North with her uncle and cousins. "Oh," she said, "you are right. I used to think that I was two-thirds Cuban; I thought I cared little, little, for the American part of me. Now—but it is music to hear you speak, Señora Carreno."

"S'pose you call me Marm Prudence!" said the good woman, half-shyly. "I don't see as 'twould be any harm, and I should like dretful well to hear the name again. I was a widow when I married Don Noonzio. Yes'm. My first husband was captain of a fruit schooner. I voyaged with him considerable. He died in Santiago, and I never went back home: I couldn't seem to. I washed and sewed for families I knew, and then bumbye I married Don Noonzio. He gave me a good home, and he's a good provider. There's times, though, that I'm terrible homesick. There! I don't know what I should do if 'twa'n't for my settin'-room. Did you notice it, comin' through? I just go there and set sometimes, and look round, and cry. It does me a sight o' good."

Rita had indeed glanced around the sitting-room as she passed through it, but it said nothing to her. The six haircloth chairs, the marble-topped centre-table with its wool and bead mat, its glass lamp with the red wick, its photograph-album and gilt family Bible, did not speak her language. Neither did the mantelpiece, with its two china poodles and its bunches of dried grasses in vases of red and white Bohemian glass. The Cuban girl could not know how eloquent were all these things to the exiled Vermont woman; but she looked sympathetic, and felt so, her heart warming to the homely soul, with her rugged speech and awkward gestures.

Marm Prudence now insisted that her guest must be tired, and brought out a superb quilt, powdered with red and blue stars, to tuck her up under; but word came that Captain Montfort was going, and Rita hurried out to the verandah to bid him farewell. Carlos took her in his arms, affectionately. "How is it, then, little sister?" he asked. "Are you reconciled at all? Can you stay here in peace a little, with these good people?"

Rita returned his caress heartily. "You were right, Carlos!" she said. "You and the dear General were both right. It was wonderful to be there in camp; I shall never forget it; I hope I shall be better all my life for it; but I could not have stayed long, I see that now. Here I shall be taken care of; here I shall rest, as under a grandmother's care. This good Marm Prudence,—that is what I am to call her, Carlos,—already I love her, already she tends me as a bird tends her young. Ah, Carlos, you will not neglect Chico? I leave him as a sacred legacy. The men implored me so. They said the bird had brought them good fortune once, and would be their salvation again; I had not the heart to take him from them. You will see that they do not feed him too much? Already he has had a fit of illness from too much kindness on the part of our faithful soldiers. Thank you! and have no thought of me, my brother; all will be well with me. Return to your glorious duty, son of Cuba. It may be that even here, in this peaceful spot, it may be given to your Rita to serve the mother we both adore. Adios, Carlos! Heaven be with thee!"

Carlos, who was of a practical turn of mind, was always uncomfortable when Rita spread her rhetorical wings. He did not see why she could not speak plain English. But he kissed her affectionately, heartily glad that he could leave her content with her surroundings; and with a cordial farewell to the good people of the house, he rode away, followed by his clanking orderlies, leading the horse Rita had ridden.

While all this had been going on, Manuela had been arranging her mistress's things; shaking out the crumpled dresses, brushing off the bits of grass and broken straw that clung to hem and ruffle, mementoes of the days in camp. Manuela sighed over these relics, and shook her head mournfully.

"Poor Pepe!" she said. "If only he does not fall into a fever from grief! Ah, love is a terrible thing! Dios! what a rent in the señorita's serge skirt! A paralysis on the brambles in that place! yet it was a good place. At least there was life. One heard voices, neighing of horses, jingling of stirrups. Here we shall grow into two young cabbages beside that old one, my señorita and her poor Manuela. Ah, life is very sad!"

Here Manuela chanced to look out of the window, and saw a handsome Creole boy leading a horse to water in the courtyard. Instantly her face lighted up. She flew to the looking-glass, and was arranging her hair with passionate eagerness, when the door opened, and Rita entered, followed by their kind hostess. Manuela started, then turned to drop a demure courtsey. "I was examining the glass," she explained, "to see if it was fit for the señorita to use. These common mirrors, you understand, they draw the countenance this way, that way,—" she expressed her meaning in vivid pantomime,—"one thinks one's visage of caoutchouc. But this is passable; I assure you, señorita, passable."

"Well, I declare!" said Marm Prudence. "My best looking-glass, that I brought from Chelsea, Massachusetts, when I was first married! If it ain't good enough for you, young woman, you're free to do without it, and so I tell you."

She spoke with some severity, but softened instantly as she turned to Rita. "Now you'll lie down and rest you a spell, won't you, dear?" she said. "I must go and see about supper, and I sha'n't be satisfied till I see you tucked up under my 'Old Glory spread.' That's what I call it; it has the colours, you see. There! comfortable? Now you shut your pretty eyes, and have a good sleep. And you," she added, turning to Manuela, "can come and help me a spell, if you've nothing better to do. I'm short-handed; help is turrible skurce in war-time, and I can keep you out of Satan's hands, if nothing else."

CHAPTER IX
IN HIDING

"You busy, Miss Margaritty?"

It was Marm Prudence's voice, and at the sound Rita opened her door quickly. She and Manuela had been holding a mournful consultation over the state of her wardrobe, which had had rough usage during the past two weeks, and she was glad of an interruption.

"I thought mebbe you'd like to come and set with me a spell while I worked."

"Oh, yes!" cried Rita, eagerly. "And may I not work, too? Isn't there something I can do to help?"

"Why, I should be pleased!" said the good woman. "I'm braidin' hats for the soldiers. I promised a dozen to-morrow night. It's pretty work; mebbe you'd like to try."

"For the soldiers? For our soldiers? Oh, what joy, Marm Prudencia! No, Prudence, you like better that. Show me, please! I burn to begin."

"Why, you're real eager, ain't you?" said Marm Prudence. "Now I'm glad I spoke; I thought mebbe 'twould suit you. Young folks like to be at something."

In a few minutes the two were seated on the cool inner verandah, looking out on the garden, with a great basket between them, heaped with delicate strips of palmetto leaf, white and smooth.

"Husband, he whittles 'em for me," Marm Prudence explained. "It's occupation for him. Fleshy as he is, he can't get about none too much, and this keeps his hands busy. It's hard to be a man and lose the activity of your limbs. But there! there's compensations, I always say. If Noonsey was as he was ten years ago, he'd be off with the rest, and then where'd I be?"

"Then"—Rita's eyes flashed, and she bent nearer her hostess, and spoke low. "Then you are not at heart pacificos, Marm Prudence. On the surface, I understand, I comprehend, it is necessary; but au fond, in your secret hearts, you are with us; you are Cubans. Is it not so? It must be so!"

"Oh, land, yes!" said Marm Prudence, composedly. "I'm an American, you see; and husband, he's a Cuban five generations back. We don't have no dealin's with the Gringos, more than we're obleeged to. Livin' right close t' the road as we do, we can't let out the way we feel, but I guess there's mighty few Mambis about here but knows where to come when they want things. There ain't many so bold as your brother, to come in open daylight, but come night, they're often as thick as bats about the garden here. There! I have to shoo' em off sometimes; yet I like to have 'em, too."

Rita's face glowed with excitement. "Oh, Marm Prudence," she cried; "how glorious! Oh, what fortune, what joy, to be here with you! We will work together; we will toil; our blood shall flow in fountains, if it is needed. Embrace me, mother of Cuba!"

Marm Prudence put on her spectacles, and surveyed the excited girl with some anxiety.

"Let me feel your pult, dear!" she said, soothingly. "You got a touch o' sun, like as not, riding in that heat this morning. Now there's no call to get worked up, or talk about blood-sheddin'. Blood-sheddin' ain't in our line, yours nor mine, nor husband's neither. Fur as doin' goes, we're all pacificos here, Miss Margaritty, and you mustn't forget that. Just wait a minute, and I'll go and git you a cup of my balm-tea; 'tis real steadyin' to the nerves, and I expect yours is strung up some with all you've be'n through."

Rita protested that she was perfectly well, and not at all excited; but she submitted, and drank the balm-tea meekly, as it was cold and refreshing.

"It is my ardent nature!" she explained. "It is the fire of my patriotism which consumes me. Do you not feel it, Marm Prudence, oftentimes, like a flame in your bosom?"

No, Marm Prudence was not aware that she did. Things took folks different, she said, placidly. She had an aunt when she was a little gal, that used to have spasms reg'lar every time she heard the baker's cart. Some thought she had had hopes of the baker before he married a widow woman, but you couldn't always account for these things. What a pretty braid Rita was getting!

Indeed, the work suited Rita's nimble fingers to perfection, and yard after yard of snowy braid rolled over her lap and grew into a pile at her feet. She was eager to make her first hat. After an hour or two of braiding, she discovered that it suited Manuela's genius better than her own. The basket of splints was turned over to the willing handmaiden, and good-natured Marm Prudence showed Rita how to sew the braids together smooth and flat, and initiated her into the mysteries of crown and brim. In a creditably short space of time, Rita, with infinite pride, held her first hat aloft, and twirled it round and round on her finger.

"But, it is perfect!" she cried. "The shape, the colour, the air of it. Manuela, quick! a mirror! hold it for me—so! look!" She took the ribbon from her belt, and began to twist it in one coquettish knot after another about the hat, which she had set on her dark hair.

"Is that chic? Is it adorable, I ask you? Was such a hat ever seen in Paris? Never! I wear no other from this day on; hear me swear it! It will become the rage; I will make it so. Or—no! I will keep to myself the secret, and others will die of envy. I name it, Manuela. The Prudencia, for thee, my kind hostess. Why do you laugh?"

Marm Prudence was twinkling in her quiet way. "I was only

thinkin' there'd have to be one soldier boy go without his hat tomorrow!" she said, good-humouredly. "It does look nice on you, though, Miss Margaritty, that's certin."

Blushing scarlet, Rita tore the hat from her head.

"Ah!" she cried, casting it on the floor. "Wretch, ingrate, serpent that I am! Take away the glass, girl! take it away; break it into a thousand pieces, to shame my vanity, and never speak to me of hats again. Henceforward I tie a shawl over my head, for the remainder of my life; I have said it."

Much depressed, she worked away in silence, as if her life depended upon it. Manuela, shrugging her shoulders, carried off the glass, but did not think it necessary to obey the injunction to break it. She was used to her señorita's outbreaks, and returned placidly to her braiding as if nothing had happened.

The good hostess regarded her pretty visitor with some alarm, mingled with amusement and admiration. She might have her hands full, she thought, if she attempted to keep this young lady occupied, and out of mischief. The time when she was asleep was likely to be the most peaceful time in Casa Annunzio. Yet how pretty she was! and what a pleasure it was to hear her speak, something between a bird and a flute. On the whole, Marm Prudence thought her coming a thing to be thankful for.

Talking with Don Annunzio himself that evening, Rita found him far less guarded than his wife in his expression of patriotic zeal. He echoed her saying, that every Mambi in the country knew where to come when he wanted anything; and he went on to draw lurid pictures of what he would do to the Gringos if he but had the power.

"See, señorita!" he said, in his wheezy, asthmatic voice. "I am powerless, am I not? Already of a certain age, I am afflicted with an accession of flesh; moreover, I am short of breath, owing to this apoplexy of an asthma. Worse than this, my legs, if the señorita can pardon the allusion, refuse now these two years to do their office. With two sticks, I can hobble about the house and garden; without them, behold me a fixture. How, then? When the war breaks out, I go to my General, to General Sevillo, under whom I served in the ten years' war. I say to him, 'Things are thus and thus with me, but still I would serve my country. Give me a horse, and let me ride with you as an orderly.' Alas! it may not be. 'Annunzio,' he says, 'your day of service in the field is over. Stay at home, and help our men when they call upon you. Thus you can do more good ten-fold than you could do in the saddle.'

"Ohimé! my heart is broken; it is reduced to powder, but what will you? reason, joined to authority,—I am but a simple man, and I obey. Since then, I sit and whittle splints for my admirable wife. A woman, señorita, to rule a nation! The Gringos pass by, and see me working at my trade. I greet them civilly, I supply requisitions when backed by authority; again, what will you? I suffer in silence till their back is turned, and my maledictions accompany them along the road. Ah! if none of them had longer life than I wish him, the road would be encumbered with corpses. Then,—draw your chair nearer, señorita, if you will have the infinite graciousness,—then, at night—it may be this very night—the others come. Hush! yes—the Mambis; the sons of Cuba. Quietly, by ones, by twos, they appear, dropping from the sky, rising from the earth. Then—ha! then, you shall see. Not a word more, Señorita Margarita! Donna Prudencia is a pearl, an empress among women, but rightly named; she complains that I talk too much on these subjects. But when one's heart is in the field, and one's legs refuse to follow,—again, what would you? No matter! silence is golden! Wait but a little, and you shall see. Who knows? It may be this very night."

Thus Don Annunzio, with many nods and winks, and gestures of dramatic caution. His words fanned the flame of Rita's zeal, and she longed for one of the promised nocturnal visits. That night and the next she was constantly waking, listening for a whisper, the clank of a chain, the jingle of a spur; but none came, and the nights passed as peacefully as the days. The dozen, and more, were completed;

and then, in spite of her vow, Rita found time to make one for herself, certainly as pretty a hat as heart could desire. So pretty, Rita thought it a thousand pities that there was no one beside Don Annunzio and Marm Prudence to see her in it. She sighed, and thought of the camp among the hills, of Carlos and the General, and Don Uberto.

One day, soon after noon, Marm Prudence asked Rita if she would like to take a walk with her. Rita assented eagerly, and put on her pretty hat. She looked on with surprise as Marm Prudence proceeded to take from a cupboard an ample covered basket, from which protruded the neck of a bottle and some plump red bananas.

"Are we going on a picnic, then?" she asked.

The good woman nodded. "You'll see, time enough!" she said. "It's a picnic for somebody, if not for us, Miss Margaritty. Look, dear! is Don Noonsey out in the ro'd there?"

Don Annunzio was out in the road, having made what was quite a journey for him, down the verandah steps, along the garden walk, and across the sunny road. He now stood shading his eyes with his hand, looking this way and that with anxious glances.

At length, "All is quiet!" he said. "The road is clear, and no sign anywhere. Make haste then, mi alma, and cross while yet all is safe."

Beckoning to Rita, Marm Prudence slipped out and across the road swiftly, not pausing till she had gained the screen of a thick clump of cacti. Rita kept close to her side, drinking the mystery like wine. They stood for a few moments behind the aloes; then Don Annunzio spoke again.

"All is still perfect, and you may go without fear. Carry my best greetings whither you are going. At the proper hour I will await you here, and signal when return is safe."

Without wasting words, his wife waved her hand, and turning, plunged into the forest, followed by the delighted Rita.

The tangle of underbrush was higher than their heads, but they made their way quickly, and Rita soon saw that a narrow path wound along through the bush, and that the ground under her feet had been trodden many times. The trees towered high above the dense undergrowth, some leafy and branching, others, the palms, tossing their single plume aloft. Open near the wood, the wood grew thicker and thicker, till it stood like a wall on either side of the narrow footpath; the twigs and leaves, broken and crushed here and there, showed, like the path, the traces of frequent passage.

Rita was burning with curiosity, yet she would not for worlds have asked a question. They were nearing every moment the heart of the mystery; she would not spoil the dramatic effect by prying into it too soon.

Suddenly, a gleam of sunlight struck through the trees. They were near the end of the wood, then. A few steps more, and she caught her breath, with a low cry of amazement.

A round hollow, dipping deep like a cup, with here and there a great tree standing. On one side, a clear spring flowing from a rocky cleft. Under one tree, a hammock slung, and in a hammock a man asleep. Thus much Rita saw at the first glance. The next instant the man was on his feet, and the long barrel of his carbine gleamed level at sight.

"Alto! quien va?" the challenge rang clear and sharp.

"Cuba!" replied Señora Carreno. "For the land's sake, Mr. Delmonty, don't start a person like that. You'd oughter know my sunbunnit by this time."

The young man had already lowered his weapon, and showed a laughing face of apology as he lifted his broad-brimmed hat.

"I beg your pardon, Donna Prudencia," he said. "I was asleep, and dreaming; not of angels!" he added, as he made another low bow, which included Rita in its sweep of respectful courtesy.

He spoke English like an Anglo-Saxon, without trace of accent or hesitation. His hair and complexion were brown, but a pair of bright blue eyes lightened his face in an extraordinary manner.

Who might this be?

"Mr. Delmonty, let me make ye acquainted with Miss Margaritty Montfort!" said Señora Carreno, with some ceremony. "Miss Montfort is stoppin' with us for a spell. Both of you bein' half Yankee, I judged you might be pleased to meet up with each other."

Rita bowed with her most queenly air; then relaxed, as she met the merry glance of the blue eyes.

"Are you?" she said. "I am very glad—but your name is Spanish."

"My father was a Cuban," said the young man; "my mother is American. She was a Russell of Claxton." He paused a moment, as if inviting comment; but Rita, brought up in Cuba, knew nothing of the Russells of Claxton, a famous family.

"I've been in the North most of the time since I was a little shaver," he went on, "at school and college; came down here last year, when things seemed to be brewing. Have you been much in Boston, Miss Montfort? We might have some acquaintances in common."

Rita shook her head, and told him of her one summer in the North. "I hope to go again," she said, "when our country is free. When Cuba has no longer need of her daughters, as well as her sons, I shall gladly return to that fair northern country."

Again she caught a quizzical glance of the blue eyes, and was reminded, she hardly knew why, of her Uncle John. But Uncle John's eyes were brown.

"You are—alone here, Señor Delmonte?" she asked, glancing around the solitary dell.

"Yes," said the young man, composedly. "I'm in hiding."

Rita's eyes flashed. Hiding! a son of Cuba! skulking about in the woods, while his brother soldiers were at the front, or, like Carlos, guarding the hill passes! This was indeed being only half a Cuban. She would have nothing to do with recreant soldiers; and she turned away with a face of cold displeasure.

"How's your foot?" asked Señora Carreno, abruptly. "That last dressing fetch it, do you think?"

"All right!" said the young man. "Look! I have my shoe on." And he held up one foot with an air of triumph. "I shall be ready for the road to-night, and take my troublesome self off your hands, Señora Carreno."

"No trouble at all!" said the good woman, earnestly. "Not a mite of trouble but what was pleasure, Captain Jack."

Captain Jack! where had Rita heard that name? Before she could try to think, her hostess went on.

"Well, I kinder hate to have you go, but of course you're eager, same as all young folks are. But look here! You'd better pass the night with us, and let me see to your foot once more, and give you a good night's sleep in a Christian bed; and then I can mend up your things a bit, and you lay by till night again, and start off easy and comfortable."

"It sounds very delightful," said the young man, with a glance at the charming girl who would stand with her head turned away. "But how about the Gringos, Donna Prudencia? Supposing some of them should come along to-morrow!"

"They won't come to-morrow!" said Marm Prudence, significantly.

72

"No? you have assurance of that? and why may they not come tomorrow?"

"Because they've come to-day, most likely!"

Rita started, and turned back toward the speakers.

"The Gringos? to-day?" she cried.

Marm Prudence nodded. "That was why I brought you here, dear," she said; "most of the reason, that is. We got word they was most likely comin', quite a passel of 'em; and we judged it was well, Don Noonsey and me, that they shouldn't see you. I thought mebbe," she added, with a sly glance at the basket, "that if I brought a little something extry, we might get an invitation to take a bite of luncheon, but we don't seem to."

"Oh! but who could have supposed that I was to have all the good things in the world?" cried Delmonte, merrily. "This is really too good to be true. Help me, Donna Prudencia, while I set out the feast! Why, this is the great day of the whole campaign."

The two unpacked the basket, with many jests and much laughter; they were evidently old friends. Meantime Rita stood by, uncertain of her own mood. To miss an experience, possibly terrible, certainly thrilling; to have lost an opportunity of declaring herself a daughter of Cuba, possibly of shooting a Spaniard for herself, and to have been deceived, tricked like a child; this brought her slender brows together, ominously, and made her eyes glitter in a way that Manuela would have known well. On the other hand—here was a romantic spot, a young soldier, apparently craven, but certainly wounded, and very good-looking; and here was luncheon, and she was desperately hungry. On the whole—

The tragedy queen disappeared, and it was a cheerful though very dignified young person who responded gracefully to Delmonte's petition that she would do him the favour to be seated at his humble board.

CHAPTER X

MANUELA'S OPPORTUNITY

That was a pleasant little meal, under the great plane-tree in the cup-shaped dell. Marm Prudence had kept, through all her years of foreign residence, her New England touch in cookery, and Señor Delmonte declared that it was worth a whole campaign twice over to taste her doughnuts. They drank "Cuba Libre" in raspberry vinegar that had come all the way from Vermont, and Rita was obliged to confess that Señor Delmonte was a charming host, and that she was enjoying herself extremely.

It was late in the afternoon when she and Marm Prudence took their way back through the forest. At first Rita was silent; but as distance increased between them and the dell, she could not restrain her curiosity.

How was it, she asked, that this young man was there alone, separated from his companions? He said he was in hiding. Hiding! a detestable, an unworthy word! Why should a son of Cuba be in hiding, she wished to know! She had worked herself into a fine glow of indignation again, and was ready to believe anything and everything bad about the agreeable youth with the blue eyes.

"I must know!" she repeated, dropping her voice to a contralto note that she was fond of. "Tell me, Marm Prudence; tell me all! have I broken the bread of a recreant?"

"I thought it was my bread," said Marm Prudence, dryly. "I'll tell you, if you'll give me a chance, Miss Margaritty. I supposed, though, that you'd have heard of Jack Delmonty; Captain Jack, as they call him. Since his last raid the Gringos have offered a big reward for him, alive or dead. He was wounded in the foot, and thought he might hender his troop some if he tried to go with them in that state. So he camped here, and we've seen to him as best we could."

Rita was dumb, half with amazement, half with mortification. How was it possible that she had been so stupid? Heard of Captain Jack? where were her wits? the daring guerrilla leader, the pride of the Cuban bands, the terror of all Spaniards in that part of the island. Why, he was one of her pet heroes; only—only she had fancied him so utterly different. The Captain Jack of her fancy was a gigantic person, with blue-black curls, with eyes like wells of black light (she had been fond of this bit of description, and often repeated it to herself), a superb moustache, and a nose absolutely Grecian, like the Santillo nose of tender memory. This half-Yankee stripling, blue-eyed, with a nose that—yes, that actually turned up a little, and the merest feather of brown laid on his upper lip—how could she or any one suppose this to be the famous cavalry leader?

Rita blushed scarlet with distress, as she remembered her bearing, which she had tried to make as scornful as was compatible with good manners. She had meant, had done her best, to show him that she thought lightly of a Cuban soldier who, for what reason soever, proclaimed himself without apology to be "in hiding." To be sure, he had not seemed to feel the rebuke as she had expected he would. Once or twice she had caught that look of Uncle John in his eyes; the laughing, critical, yet kindly scrutiny that always made her feel like a little girl, and a silly girl at that. Was that what she had seemed to Captain Delmonte? Of course it was. She had had the great, the crowning opportunity of her life, of doing homage to a real hero (she forgot good General Sevillo, who had been a hero in a quiet and business-like way for sixty years), and she had lost the opportunity.

It was a very subdued Rita who returned to the house that evening. At the edge of the wood they were met by Don Annunzio, who stood as before, smoking his long black cigar, and scrutinising the road and the surrounding country. A wave of his hand told them that all was well, and they stepped quickly across the road, and in another minute were on the verandah.

Don Annunzio followed them with an elaborate air of indifference; but once seated in his great chair, he began to speak eagerly, gesticulating with his cigar.

"Dios! Prudencia, you had an inspiration from heaven this day. What I have been through! the sole comfort is that I have lost twenty pounds at least, from sheer anxiety. Imagine that you had not been gone an hour, when up they ride, the guerrilla that was reported to us yesterday. At their head, that pestiferous Col. Diego Moreno. He dismounts, demands coffee, bananas, what there is. I go to get them; and, the saints aiding me, I meet in the face the pretty Manuela. Another instant, and she would have been on the verandah, would have been seen by these swine, female curiosity having led her to imagine a necessary errand in that direction. I seize this charming child by the shoulders, I push her into her room. I tell her, 'Thou hast a dangerous fever. Go to thy bed on the instant, it is a matter of thy life.'

"My countenance is such that she obeys without a word. She is an admirable creature! Beauty, in the female sex—"

"Do go on, Noonsey," said his wife, good-naturedly, "and never mind about beauty now. Land knows we have got other things to think about."

"It is true, it is true, my own!" replied the amiable fat man. "I return to the verandah. This man is striding up and down, cutting at my poor vines with his apoplexy of a whip. He calls me; I stand before him thus, civil but erect.

"'Have you any strangers here, Don Annunzio?'

"'No, Señor Colonel.'

"It is true, señorita. To make a stranger of you, so friendly, so gracious—the thought is intolerable.

"He approaches, he regards me fixedly.

"'A young lady, Señorita Montfort, and her maid, escaped from the carriage of her stepmother, the honourable Señora Montfort, while on the way to the convent of the White Sisters, ten days ago. A man of my command was taken by these hill-cats of Mambis, and carried to a camp in this neighbourhood. He escaped, and reported to me that a young lady and her attendant were in the camp. I raided the place yesterday.'

"'With success, who can doubt?' I said. Civility may be used even to the devil, whom this officer strongly resembled.

"He stamped his feet, he ground his teeth, fire flashed from his eyes. 'They were gone!' he said. 'They had been gone but a few hours, for the fires were still burning, but no trace of them was to be found. I found, however, in a deserted rancho,—this!' and he held up a delicate comb of tortoise-shell."

"My side-comb!" cried Rita. "I wondered where I had lost it. Go on, pray, Don Annunzio."

"He questioned me again, this colonel, on whom may the saints send a lingering disease. I can swear that there is no young lady in the house? but assuredly, I can, and do swear it, with all earnestness. He whistles, and swears also—in a different manner. He says, 'I must search the house. This is an important matter. A large reward is offered by the Señora Montfort for the discovery of this young lady.'

"'Search every rat-hole, my colonel,' I reply; 'but first take your coffee, which is ready at this moment.'

"In effect, Antonia arrives at the instant with the tray. While she is serving him, I find time to slip with the agility of the serpent into the passage, and turn the handle of the bedroom door. 'Spotted fever!' I cry through the crack; and am back at my post before the colonel could see round Antonia's broad back. Good! he drinks his coffee. He devours your cakes, my Prudencia, keeping his eye on me all the time, and plying me with questions. I tell him all is well with us, except the sickness.

"'How then? what sickness?'

"'A servant is ill with fever,' I say. 'We hope that it will not spread through the house; it is a bad time for fever.' I see he does not like that, he frowns, he mutters maledictions. I profess myself ready to conduct him through my poor premises; I lead him through the parlour, which he had not sense to admire, to the kitchen, to our own apartment, my cherished one. All the time my heart flutters like a wounded dove. I cry in my soul, 'All depends on the wit of that child. If she had but gone with Prudencia to the forest!'

"Finally there is no escape, we must pass the door. I stop before it. 'Open!' says the colonel.

"'Your Excellency will observe,' I say, 'that there is a dangerous case of spotted fever in this room.'

"He turns white, then black. He pulls his moustache, which resembles a mattress.

"At last 'How do I know?' he cries; 'You may be lying! all Cubans are liars. The girl may be in this room!'

"I throw open the door and step back, my heart in my mouth, my eyes flinging themselves into the apartment. Heavens! what do we see? a hideous face projects itself from the bed. Red—black—a face from the pit! A horrible smell is in our nostrils—we hear groans—enough! The colonel staggers back, cursing. I close the door and follow him out to the verandah. My own nerves are shaken, I admit it; it was a thing to shatter the soul. Still cursing, he mounts his horse, and rides away with his troop. I see them go. They carry away the best of what the house holds, but what of that? they are gone!

"I hasten, as well as my infirmity allows, to the chamber. I cry 'Manuela, is it thou?'

"I am bidden to enter. I open the door, and find that admirable child at the toilet-table, washing her face and laughing till the tears flow. Already half of her pretty face is clean, but half still hideous to behold.

"'How did you do it?' I ask her. She laughs more merrily than before; if you have noticed, she has a laughter of silver bells, this maiden. 'The red lip-salve,' she says, 'and a little ink. Have no fear, Don Annunzio; it was you who discovered the fever, you know.'

"'But the smell, my child? there must be something bad here, something unhealthy; a vile smell!'

"She laughs again, this child. 'I burned a piece of tortoise-shell,' she says. 'Saint Ursula forgive me, it was one of the señorita's side-combs, but there was nothing else at hand.'

"Thus then, señorita, thus, my Prudencia, has Manuela virtually saved our house and ourselves. Hasten to embrace her! I have already permitted myself the salute of a father upon her charming cheek, as simple gratitude enjoined it."

As if by magic—could she have been listening in the passage?—Manuela appeared, blushing and radiant. Donna Prudencia did not think it necessary to kiss her, but she shook her warmly by the hand, telling her that she was a good girl, and fit to be a Yankee, a compliment which Manuela hardly appreciated. As for Rita, she kissed the girl on both cheeks, and stood holding her hands, gazing at her with wistful eyes.

"Ah, Manuela," she cried; "I must not begrudge it to you. You are a heroine; you have had the opportunity, and you knew how to take it. Daughter of Cuba, your sister blesses you."

Before Manuela could reply, Donna Prudencia broke in. "There! there!" she said. "Come down off your high horse, Miss Margaritty, there's a dear; and help me to see to things. Here's Captain Delmonty coming to-night, and them chicken-thieves of Gringos have carried off every living thing there was to eat in the house."

CHAPTER XI

CAPTAIN JACK

When Jack Delmonte appeared, late in the evening, he was puzzled at the change which had come over the pretty Grand Duchess, as he had mentally nicknamed Rita. In the afternoon she had appeared, he could not imagine why, to regard him as a portion of the scum of the earth. He thought her extremely pretty, and full of charm, yet he could not help feeling provoked, in spite of his amusement, at the disdainful curl at the corners of her mouth when she addressed him. Now, he was equally at a loss to understand why or how the Grand Duchess was replaced by a gentle and tender-voiced maiden, who looked up at him from under her long curved lashes with timid and deprecatory glances. She insisted on mixing his granita herself, and brought it in the one valuable cup Marm Prudence possessed, a beautiful old bit of Lowestoft. She begged to hear from his own lips about his last raid — about all his raids. She had heard about some of them; the one where he had swum the river under fire to rescue the little lame boy; the other, when he had chased five Spaniards for half a mile, with no other weapon than a banana pointed at full cock. She even knew of some exploits that he had never heard of; and the honest captain found himself blushing under his tan, and finally changed the subject by main force. It was very pleasant, of course, to have this lovely creature hanging on his words, and supplementing them with others of her own, only too extravagantly laudatory; but a fellow must tell the truth; and — and after all, what was the meaning of it? She wouldn't look at him, three hours ago.

Had they had a gay winter in Havana? he asked. He hadn't been to a dance for forty years. Was she fond of dancing? of course she was. What a pity they couldn't — here he happened to glance at Rita's black dress, and stopped short.

"Miss Montfort, I beg your pardon! It was very stupid of me. I ran on without thinking. You are in mourning. What a brute I am!"

The tears had gathered in Rita's eyes, but now she smiled through them. "It is six months since my father died," she said. "He was the kindest of fathers, though, alas! Spanish in his sympathies."

"Your mother?" hazarded Jack, full of sympathy.

"My mother died three years ago. My stepmother—" then followed the tale of her persecution, her escape, and subsequent adventures. Captain Jack was delighted with the story.

"Hurrah!" he exclaimed. "That was tremendously plucky, you know, going off in that way. That was fine! and you got to your brother all right? I wonder—is he—are you any relation of Carlos Montfort? Not his sister? You don't mean it. Why, I was at school with Carlos, the first school I ever went to. An old priest kept it, in Plaza Nero. Carlos was a good fellow, and gave me the biggest licking once—I'm very glad we met, Miss Montfort. And—I don't mean to be impertinent, I'm sure you know that; but—what are you going to do now?"

Alas! Rita did not know. "I thought I was safe here," she said. "I was to stay here with these good people till word came from my uncle in the States, or till there was a good escort that might take me to some port whence I could sail to New York. Now—I do not know; I begin to tremble, Señor Delmonte. To-day, while Donna Prudencia and I were in the forest, a Spanish guerrilla came here, looking for me. Don Diego Moreno was in command. He is a friend of my stepmother's. I know him, a cold, hateful man. If he had found me—" she shuddered.

"I know Diego Moreno, too," said Delmonte; and his brow darkened. "He is not fit to look at you, much less to speak to you. Never mind, Miss Montfort! don't be afraid; we'll manage somehow. If no better way turns up, I'll take you to Puerto Blanco myself. Trouble is, these fellows are rather down on me just now; but we'll manage somehow, never fear! Hark! what's that?"

He leaned forward, listening intently. A faint sound was heard, hardly more than a breathing. Some night-bird, was it? It came from the fringe of forest across the road. Again it sounded, two notes, a long and a short one, soft and plaintive. A bird, certainly, thought Rita. She started as Captain Delmonte imitated the call, repeating it twice.

"Juan," he said, briefly. "Reporting for orders. Here he comes!"

A burly figure crossed the road in three strides. Three more brought him to the verandah, where he saluted and stood at attention.

"Well, Juan, where are the rest of you?"

"In the usual place, Señor Captain, four miles from here," said the orderly. "I have brought Aquila; he is here in the thicket, my own horse also. Will you ride to-night?"

"To-morrow, at daybreak, Juan. I have promised Señora Carreno to sleep one night under her roof, and convince her that my foot is entirely well. Bring Aquila into the courtyard. All is quiet in the neighbourhood?"

"All quiet, Señor Captain. Good; I bring Aquila and return to the troop. You will be with us, then, before sunrise?"

"Before sunrise without fail," said Captain Jack. "Buenos noches, Juanito!"

The trooper saluted again, and slipped back across the road; next moment he reappeared leading a long, lean, brown horse, who walked as if he were treading on eggshells. They passed into the courtyard and were seen no more, Juan making his way back to the thicket by some unseen path.

"You do not stay with us through the day then, Mr. Delmonte? I am sorry!" said Rita.

"I wish I could, indeed I do; but I must get to my fellows as soon as possible. I shall come back, though, in a day or two, and put myself and my troop at your orders, Miss Montfort. How would you like to lead a troop, like Madame Hernandez?" He laughed, but Rita's eyes flashed.

"But I would die to do it!" she cried. "Ah! Señor Delmonte, once to fight for my country, and then to die—that is my ambition."

"And you'd do it well, I am sure!" said Delmonte, warmly; "the fighting part, I mean. But nobody would let you die, Miss Montfort, it would spoil the prospect."

He spoke lightly, for heroics embarrassed him, as they did Carlos.

Soon after, Donna Prudencia appeared, with bedroom candles, and stood looking benevolently at the two young people.

"I expect you've been having a good visit," she said. "Well, there's an end to all, and it's past ten o'clock, Miss Margaritty."

Rita rose with some reluctance; nor did Captain Delmonte seem enthusiastic on the subject of going to bed.

"Such a beautiful night!" he said. "Must you go, Miss Montfort? I mustn't keep you up, of course. Good-bye, then, for a few days! I shall be gone before daybreak. I'm very glad we have met."

They shook hands heartily. Rita somehow did not find words so readily as usual. "I too am glad," she said. "It is something—I have always wished to meet the 'Star of Horsemen!'"

"Oh, please don't!" cried Jack, in distress. "That was just a joke of those idiots of mine. Good gracious! if you go to calling names, Miss Montfort, I shall not dare to come back again. Good night!"

It was long before Rita could sleep. She lay with wide-open eyes, conjuring up one scene after another, in all of which Captain Delmonte played the hero's part, and she the heroine's. He was rescuing her single-handed from a regiment of Spaniards; they were galloping together at the head of a troop, driving the Gringos like sheep before them. Or, he was wounded on the field of battle, and she was kneeling beside him, holding water to his lips, and blessing the good Cuban surgeon who had taught her bandaging in the camp among the hills. At length, hero and heroine, Cuban and Spaniard, faded away, and she slept peacefully.

"What is it? what is the matter?" Rita sprang up in her bed and listened. The sound that had awakened her was repeated: a knock at the door; a voice, low but imperative; the voice of Jack Delmonte.

"Miss Montfort! are you awake?"

"Yes; what has happened?"

"The Gringos! Dress yourself quickly, and come out. You can dress in the dark?"

"Yes; oh, yes! I will come. Manuela! wake! wake! don't speak, but dress yourself; the Spaniards are here."

Hastily, with trembling hands, the two girls put on their clothes. No thought now of how or what; anything to cover them, and that quickly. They hurried out into the passage; Delmonte stood there, carbine in hand. He spoke almost in a whisper, yet every word fell clearly on their strained ears.

"It's not Moreno; it's Velaya's guerrilla: we must get away before they fire the house. Give me your hand, Miss Montfort; you will be quiet, I know. Your maid?"

"Manuela, you will not speak!"

"No, señorita!" said poor Manuela, with a stifled sob.

"My horse is ready saddled," Delmonte went on. "If I can get you away before they see us—"

"Me! but what will become of the others?" cried Rita, under her breath. "I cannot desert Manuela and Marm Prudence—Donna Prudencia."

"I am going to save you," said Jack Delmonte, quietly. "If for no other reason, I have just given my word to Donna Prudencia. The rest—I'll get back as soon as I can, that's all I can say. Follow me! hark!"

A shot rang out; another, and another. A hubbub of voices rose within and without the house; and at the same instant a bright light sprang up, and they saw each other's faces.

Delmonte ground his teeth. "Wait!" he said; and going a little way along the passage, he peered from a window. The verandah swarmed with armed men. The door was locked and barred, but they were smashing the window-shutters with the butts of their carbines. He glanced along the passage. Inside the door stood Don Annunzio, in his vast white pajamas, firing composedly through a wicket; beside him his wife, as quietly loading and handing him the weapons. Behind them huddled the few house and farm servants, negroes for the most part, but among them was one intelligent-looking young Creole. Singling him out, Delmonte led him apart, and pointed to Manuela. "Your sister!" he said. "Your life for hers."

The youth nodded, and beckoned the frightened girl to stand beside him. Rita saw no more, for Delmonte, grasping her hand firmly, led her through the winding passage and into the inner courtyard. Pausing a moment on the verandah, they looked through the archway at one side, through which streamed a red glare. The cane patch was on fire, and blazing fiercely. The flames tossed and leaped, and in front of them men were running with torches, setting fire to sheds and out-houses. Their shouts, the crackling and hissing of the flames, the shots and cries from the front of the house, turned the quiet night wild with horror. A crash behind them told that the front door had yielded.

"It's run for it, now!" said Delmonte, quietly. "Now, then, child,— quick!"

A few steps, and they were beside the brown horse, standing saddled and bridled, and already quivering and straining to be off. Delmonte lifted Rita in his arms,—no time now for courtly mounting,—then sprang to the saddle before her. He spoke to the horse, who stood trembling, but made no motion to advance.

"Aquila, softly past the gate—then for life! good boy! Miss Montfort, put your arms around me, and hold fast. Don't let go unless I drop; then try to catch the reins, and give him his head. He knows the way."

Softly, slowly, Aquila crept to the archway. He might have been shod with velvet for any sound he made. Could they get away unseen? The men with the torches were busy at their horrid work; they could not be seen yet from the front of the house. The horse crept forward, silent as a phantom. They were clear of the archway. "Now!" whispered Delmonte. "For life, Aquila!" and Aquila went, for life.

CHAPTER XII

FOR LIFE

"If we can put the fire between us and them," said Captain Jack, "we shall get off."

For a moment it seemed as if they might do it. Already they saw the road before them, the sand glowing red in the firelight. A few more strides—Just then, a Spanish soldier came running round the corner of the burning cane-patch, whirling his blazing torch. He saw them, and raised a shout. "Alerta! alerta! fugitives! after them! shoot down the Mambi dogs!"

There was a rush to the corner where a score of horses stood tethered to the fence. A dozen men leaped into the saddle and came thundering in pursuit. Aquila gave one glance back; then stretched his long lean neck, and settled into a gallop.

Before them the road lay straight for some distance, red here in the crimson light, further on white under a late moon. On one side the woods rose black and still, on the other lay open fields crossed here and there by barbed wire fences. No living creature was to be seen on the road. No sound was heard save the muffled beat of the horse's hoofs on the sand, and behind, the shouts and cries of their pursuers. Were they growing louder, those shouts? Were they gaining, or was the distance between them widening? Rita turned her head once to look back. "I wouldn't do that!" said Delmonte, quietly. "Do you mind, Miss Montfort, if I swing you round in front of me? Don't be alarmed, Aquila is all right."

Before Rita could speak, he had dropped the reins on the horse's neck, and lifted her bodily round to the peak of the saddle before him. "I'm sorry!" he said, apologetically. "I fear it is very uncomfortable; but—I can—a—manage better, don't you see?" But to himself he was saying, "Lucky I got that done before the beggars began to shoot. Now they may fire all they like. Stupid duffer I was, not to start right."

He had felt the girl's light figure quiver as he lifted her.

"Don't be frightened, Miss Montfort," he said again. "There isn't a horse in the country that can touch Aquila when he is roused."

"I am not frightened," said Rita. "I am—excited, I suppose. It is like riding on wind, isn't it?"

It was true that she felt no fear; neither did she realise the peril of their position. It was one of the dreams come true, that was all. She was riding with Delmonte, with the Star of Horsemen. He was saving her life. They had ridden so before, often and often; only now—

Pah! a short, sharp report was heard, and a little dust whiffed up on the road beside them. Pah! pah! another puff of dust, and splinters flew from a tree just beyond them. Aquila twitched his ears and stretched his long neck, and they felt the stride quicken under them. The road rushed by; they were half-way to the turn.

"Would you like to hold the reins for a bit?" asked Delmonte. "It isn't really necessary, but—thanks! that's very nice."

What was he doing? He had turned half round in the saddle; something touched her hair—the butt of his carbine. "I beg your pardon!" said Captain Jack. "I am very clumsy, I fear."

Crack! went the carbine. Rita's ears rang with the noise; she held the reins mechanically, only half-conscious of herself. Pah! pah! and again crack! The blue rifle-smoke was in her eyes and nostrils, the Mauser bullets pattered like hail on the road; and still Aquila galloped on, never turning his head, never slackening his mighty stride, and still the road rushed by, and the turn by the hill grew nearer—nearer—

Pah! Rita felt her companion wince. His left arm relaxed its hold and dropped at his side. With his right hand he carefully replaced his carbine in its sling.

"For life, Aquila!" he said softly, in Spanish; and once more Aquila gathered his great limbs under him, and once more the terrible pace quickened.

A stone? a hole in the road? who knows? In a moment they were all down, horse and riders flung in a heap together. The horse struggled to his knees, then fell again. He screamed, an agonising sound, that in Rita's excited mind seemed to mingle with the smoke and the dust in a cloud of horror. Every moment she expected to feel the iron hoofs crashing into her, as the frenzied creature struggled to regain his footing.

Delmonte had sprung clear, and in an instant he was at Rita's side, raising her. "You are hurt? no? good! keep behind me, please."

He went to the horse, and tried to lift him, bent to examine him, and then shook his head. Aquila would not rise again; his leg was shattered. Delmonte straightened himself and looked about him. If this had happened a hundred, fifty yards back! but now the woods were gone, and on either hand stretched a bare savannah, broken only by the hateful barbed wire fences. He drew his revolver quietly. The healthy brown of his face had gone gray; his eyes were like blue steel. He looked at Rita, and met her eyes fixed on him in a mute anguish of entreaty.

"Have no fear!" he said. "It shall be as it would with my own sister. I know these men; they shall not touch you alive."

He bent once more over the struggling beast, and even in his agony Aquila knew his master, and turned his eyes lovingly toward him, expecting help; and help came.

"Good-bye, lad!" The pistol cracked, and the tortured limbs sank into quiet.

"Lie down behind him!" Delmonte commanded. "So! now, still."

He knelt behind the dead horse, facing the advancing Spaniards. The revolver cracked again, and the foremost horseman dropped, shot through the head. The troop was now close upon them; Rita could see the fierce faces, and the gleam of their wolfish teeth. Delmonte fired again, and another man dropped, but still the rest came on. There was no help, then?

Delmonte looked at Rita; she closed her eyes, expecting death. The air was full of cries and curses. But—what other sound was that? Not from before, but behind them—round the turn of the road— some one was singing! In all the hurry of her flying thoughts Rita steadied herself to listen.

"For it's whoop-la! whoop!

Git along, my little dogies;

For Wyoming shall be your new home!—

"What in the Rockies is going on here, anyhow?"

Rita turned her head. A horseman had come around the bend, and checked his horse, looking at the scene before him. A giant rider on a giant horse. The moon shone on his brown uniform, his slouched felt hat, and the carbine laid across his saddle-bow. Under the slouched hat looked out a bronzed face, grim and bearded, lighted by eyes blue as Delmonte's own.

Rita gave one glance. "Help!" she cried, "America, help!"

"America's the place!" said the horseman. He waved his hand to some one behind him, then put his horse to the gallop. Next instant he was beside them.

Delmonte started to his feet, revolver in hand. "U. S. A.?" he said. "You're just in time, uncle. I'm glad to see you."

"Always like to be on time at a party," said the rough rider, levelling his carbine. "My fellows are—in short, here they are!"

There was a scurry of hoofs, a shout, and thirty horsemen swept around the curve and came racing up.

"What's up, Cap'n Jim?" cried one. "Have we lost the fun? Gringos, eh? hooray!"

The Spaniards had checked their horses. Four of them lay dead in the road, and several others were wounded. At sight of the mounted troop, they stopped and held a hurried consultation, then turned their horses and rode away.

The giant looked at Delmonte. "Want to follow?" he asked. "This is your hand, comrade."

"I want a horse!" said Captain Jack. "Miss Montfort,"—he turned to Rita, who had risen to her feet, and stood pale but quiet,—"these are our own good country-men. If I leave you with them but a few moments—"

"Hold on!" said the big man. "What did you call the young lady?"

Delmonte stared. "This is Miss Montfort," he said, rather formally.

"Not Rita!" cried the giant. "Pike's Peak and Glory Gulch! Don't tell me it's Rita!"

"Oh, yes! yes!" cried Rita, running forward with outstretched hands. "It is—I am! and you—oh, I know, I know. You are Peggy's big brother. You are Cousin Jim!"

"That's what they said when they christened me!" said Cousin Jim.

CHAPTER XIII

mEETINGS AND GREETINGS

It was no time for explanations. Jim Montfort put out a hand like a pine knot, and gave Rita's fingers a huge shake.

"Glad to find you, cousin," he said. "I've been looking for you. Now, what's up over there?" He nodded in the direction of the fire.

"A candela," said Delmonte, briefly. "I must get back; there are women there. If one of your men will catch me that horse—"

"But you are wounded!" cried Rita. "Cousin, he is shot in the arm. Do not let him go!"

Delmonte laughed. "It's nothing, Miss Montfort," he said; "but nothing at all, I assure you. When we get to camp you shall put some carbolic acid on it, and tie it up for me; that's field practice in Cuba. I shall be proud to be your first field patient." He spoke in his usual laughing way; but suddenly his face changed, and he leaned toward her swiftly, his hand on the horse's mane. "I shall never forget this time—our ride together," he said. "I hope you will not forget either—please? And now, Miss Montfort, I have no further right over you. I would have done my best, I think you know that; but—I must give you into your cousin's protection. You will remain here?"

"Of course she will!" said Cousin Jim, who had heard only the last words. "I'll go with you, comrade. Raynham, Morton, you will mount guard by the lady."

The troopers saluted, and raised their hats civilly to Rita, inwardly cursing their luck. Because they owned the next ranch to Jim Montfort, was that any reason why they should lose all the fun? and why could not girls stay at home where they belonged?

But Rita herself cried out and clasped her hands, and ran to her cousin. "Oh, Cousin Jim—Señor Delmonte—let me go with you! Please, please let me go back. My poor Manuela—Marm Prudence—they may be hurt, wounded. There can be no danger with all these brave men. Cousin, I have been in a camp hospital, I know how to dress wounds. I can be quiet—Señor Delmonte, tell him I can be quiet!"

She looked eagerly at Delmonte.

"I can tell him that you are the bravest girl I ever saw," he said. "But, you have been through a great deal. I don't like to have you go back among those rascals."

James Montfort stroked his brown beard thoughtfully.

"Guess it's safe enough," he said at last. "Guess there's enough of us to handle 'em. Don't know but on the whole she'll be better off with us. My sister Peggy wouldn't like to miss any circus there was going, would she, little girl? Catch another of those beasts for the lady, Bill!"

Rita, with one of her quick gestures, caught his great hand in both hers. "Oh, you good cousin!" she cried. "You dear cousin! You are the very best and the very biggest person in the world, and I love you."

"Well, well, well!" said Cousin Jim, somewhat embarrassed. "There, there! so you shall, my dear; so you shall. But as for being big, you should see Lanky 'Liph of Bone Gulch. Now there—but here is your horse, missy."

The horses of the dead Spaniards had been circling about them, more or less shyly. Two of them were quickly caught by the rough riders, and Rita and Delmonte mounted. As they did so, both glanced toward the spot where lay the brave horse that had borne them so well.

"It was for life indeed, Aquila!" said Captain Jack, softly. His eyes met Rita's, and she saw the brightness of tears in them. Next moment they were galloping back to the residencia.

They came only just in time. Not ten minutes had passed since they left the courtyard, but in that time the savage Spaniards had done their work well. The house itself was in flames, and burning fiercely. Good Don Annunzio lay dead, carbine in hand, on the steps of his ruined home. Beside him lay the Creole youth in whose charge Delmonte had left Manuela. The lad was still alive, for as Delmonte bent from the saddle above him he raised his head.

"I did my best, my captain!" he said. "They were too many."

"Where are they?" asked Delmonte and Montfort in one breath.

The boy pointed down the road; raised his hand to salute, and fell back, dead.

Now again it was a ride for life—not their own life this time. Rita had clean forgotten herself. The thought of her faithful friend and servant in the hands of the merciless Spaniards turned her quick blood to fire. She galloped steadily, her eyes fixed on the cloud of dust only a few hundred yards ahead of them, which told where the enemy was galloping, too.

Jim Montfort glanced at her, and nodded to himself. "She'll do!" he said in his beard. "Montfort grit's good grit, and she's got it. This would be nuts to little Peggy."

Jack Delmonte, too, looked more than once at the slender figure riding so lightly between him and the big rough rider. How beautiful she was! He had not realised half how beautiful till now. What nerve! what steadiness! It might be the Reina de Cuba, Donna Hernandez herself, riding to victory.

He felt an unreasonable jealousy of "Cousin Jim." Half—nay! a quarter of an hour ago, she was riding with him; there were only they two in the world, they and Aquila, poor Aquila,—who had given his life for theirs. She was his comrade then, his charge, his—

and now she was Miss Montfort, a young lady of fortune and position, under charge of her cousin, a Yankee captain of rough riders; and he, Jack Delmonte, was—nothing in particular.

As he was thinking these thoughts, Rita chanced to turn her head, and met his gaze fixed earnestly upon her. She blushed suddenly and deeply, the lovely colour rising in a wave over cheeks and forehead; then turned her head sharply away.

"Now I have offended her!" said Jack. "Idiot!" and perhaps he was not very wise.

But there was little time for thinking or blushing. The Spaniards, seeing Delmonte, whom they regarded as the devil in person, descending upon them in company with a giant and an army (for so they described the band of rough riders at headquarters next day), abandoned their prisoners. The Americans chased them for a mile or so, killed three or four, and, as they reported, "scared the rest into Kingdom Come," leaving them only on coming to a thick wood, into which the Gringos, leaping from their horses, vanished, and were seen no more. The victors then returned to the forlorn little group of women and negroes, huddled together by the roadside. Rita had already dismounted, and had Manuela in her arms. She felt her all over, hurrying question upon question.

"My child, you are not hurt? not wounded? these ruffians—did they dare to touch you? did they have the audacity to speak to you, Manuela? Oh, why did I leave you? I could not help it; you saw I could not help it. You are sure you have no hurt?"

"But, positively, señorita," said Manuela. "See! not a scratch is on me. They—one fellow—offered to tie my hands; I scratched him so well that he ran away. I am safe, safe—praise be to all saints, to our Holy Lady, and the Señor Delmonte. But—poor Cerito, señorita? what of him? he was with us; he fought like a lion. I saw him fall—"

"Poor Cerito!" said Rita, gravely. "He was a brave, brave lad. A thousand sons to Cuba like him!"

Donna Prudencia was sitting apart on a stone by the roadside. Rita went up to her, took her hand, and kissed her cheek. The Yankee woman looked kindly at her and nodded comprehension, but did not speak. Rita stood silent for a few minutes, timidly stroking the brown cheek and white hair. Her cousin Margaret came into her mind. What would Margaret say, if she were here? She would know the right word, she always did.

"Marm Prudence," she said, presently, "to have the memory of a hero, of one who dies for his country,—that is something, is it not? some little comfort?"

Marm Prudence did not answer at once.

"Mebbe so," she said, presently. "Mebbe so, Miss Margaritty. Noonzio was a good man. Yes'm, I've lost a good husband and a good home! A good husband and a good home!" she repeated. "That's all there is to it, I expect." Her rugged face was disturbed for a moment, and she hid it in her hands; when she looked up, she was her own composed self.

"And what's the next thing?" she asked. "Thank you, Cap'n Delmonty, I'm feeling first-rate. Don't you fret about me. You done all you could. I'll never forget what you done. Poor husband's last words before he was shot was thanking the Lord Miss Margaritty was off safe. We knew we could trust her with you."

"Indeed," said honest Delmonte, "it is not me you must thank, Donna Prudencia. I did what I could, but it was Captain Montfort and his men who saved both her life and mine."

He told the story briefly, and Marm Prudence listened with interest. "Well," she said, "that was pretty close, wasn't it? Anyway, you done all you could, Cap'n Jack, and nobody can't do no more. And he's Miss Margaritty's cousin, you say? I want to know! He's big enough for three, ain't he?"

Rita laughed, in spite of herself. She beckoned to Cousin Jim, who came up and shook hands with the widow with grave sympathy. But he seemed preoccupied, and, while they were preparing to return to the ruined farm, he was pulling his big beard and meditating with a puzzled air.

"Look here!" he broke out at last, addressing his men. "I've been wondering what was wrong. I couldn't seem to round up, somehow, and now I've got it. Where's that poor old Johnny? I left him with you when I rode forward to reconnoitre."

The rough riders looked at one another, and hung their heads.

"Guess he must have dropped behind," said Raynham. "We didn't wait long after you signalled to us to come on. We—came."

"That's so!" clamoured the rough riders, in sheepish chorus. "We came, Cap'n Jim. That's a fact!"

"Well—that's all right!" said Jim. "You might have brought the old Johnny along, though, seems to me. Two of you ride back and get him; you, Bill, and Juckins. If he seems used up, Juckins can carry him, pony and all."

Juckins, a huge Californian, second only to Montfort in stature, chuckled, and rode off with Raynham at a hand gallop.

Montfort turned to Rita.

"I haven't had time to tell you about it before," he said. "Cousin Rita, I've been hunting for you for three days. We met an old Johnny—an old gentleman, I should say—riding about on a pony, for all the world like Yankee Doodle. He'd got lost, poor old duffer, among these inferior crossroads, and didn't know whether he was in China or Oklahoma. We picked him up, and, riding along, it came out that he was searching for his ward, a young lady who had run away from a convent. Ever heard of such a person, missy? He had started out alone, to ride about Cuba till he found her. Kind of pocket Don Quixote, about five foot high, white hair, silk clothes; highly respectable Johnny."

"Don Miguel!" cried Rita. "Poor, dear, good Don Miguel! I have never written to him, wicked that I am. Oh, where is he, Cousin Jim?"

"Come to ask him," Jim continued, "it appeared that the young lady's name was Montfort. Now, I had just had a letter from Uncle John, wanting me to raise the island to get hold of you and ship you North at once. He had had no letters; was alarmed, you understand. Laid up with a bad knee, or would have come himself. I was just going to start back to the city in search of you, when up comes Don Quixote. When he heard I was your cousin, he fell into my arms, pony and all. Give you my word he did! Almost lost him in my waistcoat pocket. I cheered him up a bit, and we've been poking about together these three days, looking for General Sevillo's camp. Thought you might be there. We were camping by the roadside when we heard your firing. Ah! here he comes now!"

The rough riders came back, their horses trotting now, instead of galloping. Between them, ambling gently along, was a piebald pony of amiable appearance, and on the pony sat a little old gentleman with snow-white hair and a face as mild and gentle as the pony's own. At sight of Rita running to meet him, he uttered a cry of joy, and checked his horse. Next moment he had dismounted, and had her in his arms, sobbing like a child.

"Dear Donito Miguelito!" cried Rita. "Forgive me! please do forgive me, for frightening you. I could not go to the convent, indeed I could not. I am a wretch to have treated you so, but I could not go to that place."

"Of course you could not, my child," said the good old man. "Nunc dimittis, Domine! Now lettest thou thy servant depart in peace. Of course you could not."

"I could not live with Concepcion; don't you know I could not, Donito Miguelito?"

"The thought is impossible, my Pearl. Speaking with all possible respect, the Señora Montfort, though high-born and accomplished, is a hysterical wildcat. You did well, my child; you did extremely well. So long as I have found you, nothing matters; but, nothing at all. As my great, my gigantic friend, my colossal preserver, el Capitan Gimmo, says, 'Ourrah for oz!'"

"Hurrah!" shouted the rough riders.

CHAPTER XIV
ANOTHER CAMP

They made but a brief halt at the ruined farm. The house was completely gutted; the widow of Don Annunzio had the clothes she stood in, and nothing beside. She stood quietly by while her husband's body was laid in the grave beside that of young Cerito; a shallow grave, hastily dug in what had lately been the garden. She listened with the same quiet face while good old Don Miguel, with faltering voice, recited a Latin prayer. She was a Methodist, he a fervent Catholic; but it mattered little at that moment.

By this time it was daylight. A small patch of bananas was found, that had escaped the destroying torch, and on these the party made a hasty meal; then they rode away, all save the negroes, who preferred to stay in the neighbourhood where their lives had been spent.

They rode slowly, in deference to Don Miguel's age and that of his pony. Rita, riding beside the good old man, listened to the recital of his terrors and anxieties from the time her flight was discovered to the present moment. These caused her real grief, and she begged again and again for the forgiveness which he assured her was wholly unnecessary. But when he described the hysterical rage of her stepmother, her eyes brightened, and the colour came back to her pale cheek. She had no doubt that Concepcion Montfort was sorry to lose her; the larger part of her father's fortune had been settled upon her, Rita, before his second marriage.

"The señora also has made diligent search for you, my child!" said Don Miguel. "She has offered ample rewards—"

"I know it!" said Rita. "Only yesterday—can it be that it was only yesterday?—Don Diego Moreno was here—there, I should say, at that peaceful home that is now a heap of ashes. These Spaniards!"

Had she seen Don Diego? the old man asked; and he seemed relieved when she answered in the negative.

"It is well; it is well!" he said. "He is a relative of the señora's, I am aware; but it would have been unsuitable, most unsuitable."

"What would have been unsuitable, Donito Miguelito?"

Don Miguel looked confused. "A—nothing, my child. The Señora Montfort had an idea—Don Diego made certain advances—in short, he would have asked for your hand, my señorita—well, my Margarita, if you will have it so. But I took it upon myself to refuse these overtures without consulting you."

Rita heard a low exclamation, and turning, saw Delmonte's face like dark fire beside her.

"I beg your pardon!" he said. "I could not help hearing. Don Miguel, if Diego Moreno makes any more such proposals, kindly let me know, and I'll shoot him at sight."

"I—thank you! thank you, my son!" said Don Miguel, somewhat fluttered. "I hope no violence will be necessary. I used strong language, very strong language, to Don Diego Moreno. I—I told him that I considered him a person entirely objectionable, unfit to sweep the road before the Señorita Montfort's feet. He went away very angry. I thought we should hear no more of him; but it seems that he still retains his presumptuous idea. Without doubt, it will be best, my dear child, for you to seek the northern home of your family without delay."

Why, at this obviously sensible remark, should Rita feel a sinking at the heart, and a sudden anger against her dear old friend? And again, why, on stealing a glance at Delmonte, and seeing the trouble reflected in his face, should her heart as suddenly spring up again, and dance within her? What had happened?

They had ridden some miles, when Jim Montfort, on his big gray horse, ranged alongside of Delmonte.

"It appears to me," he said, "that something is going on in these woods here. I've seen two or three bits of brown that weren't bark, and if I didn't catch the shine of a gun-barrel just now, you may call me a Dutchman. I think I'll fire, and see what happens."

"No, don't do that!" said Delmonte, quietly. "It's only my fellows. They've been keeping alongside for the last half-mile, waiting for a signal. They might as well come out now."

He gave a low call in two notes; the call Rita had heard—was it only the night before? it seemed as if a week had passed since then.

The call was answered from the wood; and as if by magic, from every tree, from every clump of bushes, came stealing lean brown figures, leading equally lean horses, all armed and on the alert. They saluted, and, at a word from the burly Juan, fell into order with the precision of a troop on drill.

"What's all this, Juan?" asked Delmonte. "No order was given."

Juan replied with submission that a negro boy had brought news an hour ago that Don Annunzio's house had been burned, he and his whole household murdered, and their captain taken prisoner; and that the latter was being brought in irons along the road to Santiago. They, Juan and the rest, had planned a rescue, and disposed themselves to that end in the most advantageous manner. That they were about to fire, when they recognised their captain's escort as Americans; and that they then resolved to accompany the party as quietly as might be till they came near the camp, and then make their presence known to all, as they had at once made it known to Delmonte himself by a low call which only he had noticed.

"Not wishing to intrude," Juan concluded, with a superb salute.

Delmonte turned to his companions. "Miss Montfort," he said, "Captain Montfort—you'll all come up to my place, of course, and rest, for to-day, at least. It isn't much of a place to ask you to, but—

it's quiet, at least, and—you can rest; and you must be half-starved. I know I am."

His face was eager as a boy's. Rita's was not less so, as she gazed at the big cousin, who stroked his beard as usual, and reflected.

"I did mean to push straight on to Santiago," he said, "but—it's a good bit of a way, to be sure; what do you say, little cousin? tired? hey?"

Rita blushed. "A—a little tired, Cousin Jim; and very hungry!"

This settled it. Captain Montfort bid Delmonte "fire away." The latter said a few rapid words to Juan, and the scout shot off like an arrow across the fields, riding as if for his life.

An hour later, the whole party was seated around a fire, in as comfortable a nook of the hills as guerilla leader could desire, sipping coffee, and eating broiled chicken and fried bananas, fresh from the parilla. The fire was built against a great rock that rose abruptly from the dell, forming one side of it, and towering so high that the smoke disappeared before it reached the top. Thick woods framed the other sides of the natural fastness, and here the Cuban riders could lie hidden for days and weeks, unsuspected, unseen, save by the wandering birds that now and then circled above their heads. No tents or huts here; the horses were tethered to trees; the commander's hammock was swung in a shady thicket near the great rock; as for his men, a ragged blanket and the "soft side of a stone" were all they asked.

Rita had dressed Captain Delmonte's wound, and bandaged the arm in approved style, Cousin Jim looking on with grunts of approval. He and Delmonte himself both assured her that, if they were handling it, they should simply squirt carbolic acid into it, and tie it up with anything that came handy; but Rita shook her head gravely, and three of her delicate handkerchiefs, brought from the long-suffering bag which Manuela had somehow managed to save from the ruins, torn into strips, made a very sufficient bandage. The wound was, in truth, slight. Delmonte looked almost as if he wished it more severe, for the whole matter of bathing and dressing could not be stretched beyond ten minutes; but Rita's pride in her neat bandage was pretty to see, and he watched her with delighted eyes through every stage.

"Snug quarters!" said Jim Montfort, approvingly, as, the breakfast over, he stretched his huge length along the grass and looked about him; and all the party echoed his opinion. The two captains fell into talk of the war and its ways, while the women, wearied out, rested after their long night of distress and fatigue. Marm Prudence chose the dry grass, with a cloak for a pillow, but Rita curled herself thankfully in Captain Jack's hammock, after trying in vain to persuade him that he was an invalid, and ought to take it himself. After some rummaging in a hole in the rock which served him for cupboard and wardrobe, Delmonte brought her a small pillow in a somewhat weather-beaten cover. "I wish I had a better one," he said. "This has been out in the rain a good deal, and I'm afraid it smells of smoke, but it's a great pillow for sleeping on."

"Oh, thank you!" said Rita. "It is very comfortable indeed. How good you are to me, Captain Delmonte. And whatever you may say, it is a great shame for me to take your own hammock. If there were only another—"

"Oh, please don't!" said Jack. "It's really—you must not talk so, Miss Montfort. As if there was anything I wouldn't do—why, this hammock will never be the same again. I—I mean—oh, you know what I mean, and I never could make pretty speeches. But—it is a pleasure, and—an honour, to have you here; and you can't think how much it means to me. Good night! I mean—sleep well."

He added a few words of a German song relative to the desirability of a certain lovely angel's slumbering sweetly. Rita did not understand German, but the tone of Delmonte's voice was in no particular language, and, tired as she was, it was some time before she went to sleep.

It was late afternoon when they took the road again. Before starting they held a council, seated together beneath the great tree, under whose shade Rita had slept peacefully for several hours. Jim Montfort was the first speaker.

"I take it," he said, "we'd better, each one of us, say what we mean to do. Then the sky will be clear, and we can fit in or shake apart, as seems best in each case. We all ride together to Pine del Rio, as Captain Delmonte is so friendly as to ride with us. After that—I'll begin with you, ma'am." He addressed the widow respectfully. "How can I best serve you? I am going to see my cousin safe off, and you must call upon me for any service I can possibly render you."

"She will stay with me!" cried Rita. "Dear Marm Prudence, you will stay with me, will you not?"

Marm Prudence shook her head, though with a look of infinite kindliness. "Thank you, dear," she said; "it's like you to say it, but I'm going home to Greenvale, Vermont. I've a sister living there yet. I'll go back to my own folks at last, and lay my bones alongside o' mother's. I'll never forgit you, though, Miss Margaritty," she added, "nor you, Cap'n Jack. There! I can't say much yet."

She turned away, and all were silent for a moment, as she wiped the tears from her rugged face.

"You go straight home, I suppose, sir?" said Jim, addressing Don Miguel.

"Yes, yes!" cried the little gentleman. "I go to Pine del Rio with my dear ward here. To see her safe on board a good vessel, bound for the North; to say farewell to the joy of my old days, and put out the light of my eyes—that is my one sad desire, Señor Montfort. After that—I am old, I have but a short time left, and my prayers will require that."

"Well, then, it seems as if the first thing on all hands was to find a steamer sailing for home," said Jim. "If Mrs. Annunzio will take charge of you, Cousin Rita, I think that will be the best thing. Uncle John will send some one to meet you in New York and take you to Fernley. How does that suit you?"

Rita was silent. She had grown very pale. Delmonte looked at her eagerly, but did not speak.

"What do you say, little cousin?" repeated Montfort. "You have a mind of your own, and a pretty decided one, if I'm not mistaken. Let's hear it!"

Rita spoke slowly and with difficulty, her ready flow of speech lacking for once.

"Cousin Jim—dear Don Miguel—you are both so kind, so good. You too, Marm Prudence. I love the North. I love my dear uncle and cousin—ah, how dearly!—but—I do not want to go to Fernley."

"Not want to go!" repeated the others.

"No! indeed, indeed, I cannot go. I have been thinking, Cousin Jim, a great deal, while all these things have been happening; these wonderful, terrible things. I—I ought to have learned a great deal; I hope I have learned a little. I have talked enough about helping my country; too much I have talked; now I want to do something. I am going to work in one of the hospitals. Nurses are needed, I know, every day more of them. I do not know enough—yet—to be a nurse, but I can be a helper. I am very humble; I will do the meanest work, but—but that is what I mean to do."

She ceased, and all the others, looking in her face, saw it bright and lovely with earnest resolve. But Don Miguel cried out in expostulation. It was impossible, he said. It could not be. She was too young, too delicate, too—the proposition was monstrous. He appealed to Captain Montfort to support him, to exercise his authority, to persuade this dear child that the noble idea which filled her young and ardent heart was wholly impracticable.

Jim Montfort was silent for a time, looking at Rita from under his heavy eyebrows. Presently—"You mean it?" he said.

"I mean it with all my heart!" said Rita.

"Well," said Jim, "my opinion is—considering my sister Peggy and her views, to say nothing of Jean and Flora—my opinion is, Rita—hurrah for you!"

A month ago, Rita would have gone into violent heroics at such a moment as this. As it was, she smiled, though her eyes filled with tears, and said, quietly, "Thank you, cousin! It is what I expected from Peggy's brother."

"May I speak?" said another voice. They turned, and saw Jack Delmonte, his blue eyes alight with eager gladness.

"If—if Miss Montfort has this noble desire to help in the good cause," he said, "it is easy for her to do it. My mother has turned her residencia, just outside the city, into a hospital. I am going there today. She needs more help, I know. You—you would like my mother, Miss Montfort; everybody likes my mother. She would do all she could to make it easy for you, and she would be so glad—oh, I can't tell you how glad she would be. And I think you are quite certain to like her."

"Ah!" said Rita. "Have I not heard of the Saint of Las Rosas? There is no need to tell me how good and how noble the Señora Delmonte is. But—but will she like me, Captain—Captain Jack?"

"Will she?" said Jack. "Will the sun shine?"

CHAPTER XV

A FOREGONE CONCLUSION

Las Rosas, June —, 1898.

Dear Uncle John:—Since I last wrote you, telling of our finding Rita, and of her safe delivery to Señora Delmonte, things have been happening. In the first place, I got a shot in my leg, in a skirmish, and, as the bone was broken, and it didn't seem to come round as it ought, I came here to be coddled, and am having a great time of it. Señora Delmonte is a fine woman, sir. You don't see many such women in a lifetime. She has a little hospital here, as complete as if she had New York City in her back dooryard; all her own place, you understand. Kind of Florence Nightingale woman. What's more, little Rita promises to become her right hand; if she's given a chance, that is—I'll come to that by and by, though. The way that little girl takes hold, sir, is a caution. She's quick, and she's quiet, and she's cheerful; and she has brains in her head, which is a mighty good thing in a woman when you do find it. She and Señora Delmonte are like mother and daughter already; and this brings me to something else I want to say. It's pretty clear that Jack Delmonte has lost his heart to this little girl of ours. It began, I suspect, the night he carried her off from the Spaniards; you have heard all about that; and it's been going on here, while a little flesh wound he had was healing. Yes, sir, he's in it deep, and no mistake; and, for that matter, I guess she is, too, though those things aren't in my line. Anyhow, what I want to say is this: Jack Delmonte is as fine a fellow as there is this side of the Rockies; and I don't know that I'll stop there, barring my brother Hugh. This war isn't going to last much longer. By some kind of miracle, this place—sugar plantation, and well paying in good times—hasn't been meddled with; and Jack ought to be able to support a wife, if he puts good work into the business, as he will. He's a first-rate all-round fellow, and has brains in his head—said that before, didn't I? well, it's a good thing in a man, too. I'm not much of a hand at writing, as I guess you'll see. All I mean to say is, if he and little Rita want to hitch up a double team, my opinion is it would be a mighty good thing, and I hope you'll give them your blessing and all that sort of thing, when the time comes.

Much obliged for your letter, but sorry your knee still bothers you. Father has been laid up, too, so he writes; rheumatism. I'm getting on first-rate, and shall be out of this soon. I think a month or so more will see the whole blooming business over, and peace declared. Time, too! this is no kind of a country to stay in.
Your affectionate nephew,

James Montfort.

P.S. Tell Cousin Margaret that J. D. is all right.

Las Rosas, June —, 1898.

My Dear Mr. Montfort:—I wonder if you remember Mary Russell, with whom you used to dance now and then when you came to Claxton in the old days, we will not say how many years ago. I certainly have not forgotten the pleasant partner who waltzed so well, and I am glad to have the opportunity of claiming acquaintance with you. I meant to write as soon as your niece arrived at my house, but the battle in this neighbourhood the day after brought us such an influx of wounded that my hands were very full, and the hasty dictated line was all I could manage. We are now in a little eddy of the storm (which, we hope, is nearly over), and have only a dozen men in the house, and most of these convalescent; so I must not delay longer in assuring you of the very great pleasure and help it has been to me to have Margarita with me. Indeed, I hardly know what I should have done without her the first week, as two of my nurses were ill just at the time when we were fullest. She shows a remarkable aptitude for nursing, which is rather singular, as she tells me that until lately she has been extremely timid about such matters, fainting at the sight of blood, etc. You never would think it now, to see her going about her work in the wards. The patients idolise her, and what is more (and less common), so do the nurses, who declare that she will miss her vocation if she does not go into a training-school as soon as she leaves Las Rosas; but I fancy you would not choose so arduous a life for her.

This brings me, my dear Mr. Montfort, to what is really the chief object in my writing to you to-day. Without beating about the bush, I am going to say, at once and frankly, that my dear son, Jack, has become deeply attached to this charming niece of yours. Who could be surprised at it? she must always have been charming; but the sweetness and thoughtfulness that I have seen growing day by day while she has been under my charge are, I somehow fancy, a new phase of her development. Indeed, Rita herself has told me, in her vivid way, of some of the wild pranks of her "unguided youth," as she calls it,—the child will be nineteen, I believe, on her next birthday!—and we have laughed and shaken our heads together over them. She is far more severe upon herself than I can be, for I see the quick, impulsive nature, and see, too, how it is being subdued and brought more and more under control by a strong will and a good heart. A very noble woman our Rita will make, if she has the right surroundings.

Can we give her these? that is the question; a question for you to answer, dear Mr. Montfort. Jack saw readily, when I pointed it out to him, that it would not be suitable for him to speak of love to an orphan girl—an heiress, too, I believe—without her guardian's express consent. He chafes at the delay, for he is very ardent, being half Cuban; but you may have entire confidence that he will say nothing to Rita until I hear from you.

You can easily find out about Jack; there is nothing in his life that he need conceal. Colonel G. and Mrs. B——, in New York, Professor Searcher and Doctor Lynx, of Blank College, will tell you of his school and college days; and Captain Montfort will, I think, say a good word for his record as a soldier and a patriot. Of course, in my eyes, he is a little bit of a hero; but maternal prejudice laid aside (if such a thing may be!), I can truly say that he is a clean, honest, high-minded man, with a sound constitution and an excellent disposition. Add to this a moderate income (not, I am happy to say, enough to allow him to dispense with work, were he inclined to do so, which he is not), and a very earnest and devoted attachment, and you have the whole case before you. May I hope to have your answer as soon as you shall have satisfied yourself on the various points on which you will naturally seek information? I assure you that, with the best intentions in the world, Jack does find it hard to restrain himself. Let me add that, if your answer is favourable, it will make me as well as my son very happy. Rita is all that I could wish for in a daughter; and I shall try my best to fill a mother's place toward her.

In any case, believe me, dear Mr. Montfort,
Cordially yours,

Mary Russell Delmonte.

P.S. You may ask, does Rita return Jack's affection? I think she does!

Santiago, June —, 1898.

Honoured Señor:—Your valued letter, containing inquiries on the subject of Señor Captain John Delmonte is at hand and contents notified. I hasten to reply with all the ardour of which I am capacious. This young man is a nobleman; few princes have equalled him in virtuous worth. Brave, honourable, pious (though Protestant; but this belief is probably your own, and is held by many of those most valuable to me, your honoured brother among them), a faithful and obedient son, a leader beloved to rapture by his soldiers. If more could be to say, I would hasten to cry it aloud. You tell me, with noble frankness, he is a pretender for the hand of my beloved Margarita; already it has been my happiness to be aware of it. Señor Montfort, to see these two admirable young persons united in the holy bondages of weddinglock is the last and chief wish of my life. I earnestly beg your sanction of their unition. In Jack I find a son for my solitary age; in Margarita a daughter, the most tender as she is the most beautiful that the world contains. To close my aged eyes on seeing them unified, is, I repeat it, the one wish of,

Honoured Señor,

Your most obedient and humble servitor,

Miguel Pietoso.

Las Rosas, June —, 1898.

My Dear Mr. Monfort:—I have just read your letter to my mother, and I want to thank you before I do anything else. There isn't much to say, except that I will do my best to be in some degree worthy of this treasure, if I win it. I will try to make her happy, sir, I will indeed. No one could be good enough for her, so I will not pretend to that.

She is awake now, so I must go.

Gratefully yours,

John Delmonte.

Las Rosas, Evening.

Dearest, dearest Margaret:—Why are you not here? I want you—oh, I want you so much! I am so happy, so wonderfully, almost terribly happy, how can I put it on paper? The paper will light itself, will burn up for joy, I think; but I will try. Listen! an hour ago—it is an evening of heaven, the moon was shining for me, for me and—oh, but wait! I was in the garden, resting after the day's work; I had been asleep, and now would take the remainder of my free time in waking rest. The air was balm, the roses all in blossom. Such roses were never seen, Marguerite; the place is named for them, Las Rosas. They are in bowers, in garlands, in heaps and mounds—I smell them now. The rose is my flower, remember that, my life long. I used to tell you it was the jessamine; the jessamine is a simpleton, I tell you. I was picking white roses, the kind that blushes a little warm at its heart—when I heard some one coming. I knew who it was; can I tell how? It was Captain Jack. I trembled. He came to me, he spoke, he took my hand. Oh, my dear, my dear, I cannot tell you what he said; but he loves me; he is my Jack, I am his Rita. Marguerite, will you tell me how it can be true? Your wild, silly, foolish Rita, playing at emotions all her childish life: she wakes up, she begins to try to be a little like you, my best one; and all of a sudden she finds herself in Paradise, with a warrior angel—Marguerite, I did not think of it till this moment; my Jack is the express image of St. Michael. His nose tips up the least bit in the world—I don't mind it; it gives life, dash, to his wonderful face; otherwise there is no difference. My St. Michael! my soldier, my Star of Horsemen! Marguerite, no girl was ever so happy since the world was made. Oh, don't think me fickle; let me tell you! In the South here, are we different? It must be so. I was fond of Santayana; but that was in another life. I was a sentimental, passionate child; he was handsome as a picture; it was a dream of seventeen. Now—can you believe that I am a little grown up? I really think I am. Perhaps I think it most because now, for the first time, I really want to be like you, Marguerite. I used to be so pleased with being myself—I was the vainest creature that ever lived. Now, I want to be like you instead; I want to be a good woman, a good wife. Ah! what a wife you will make if you marry! But how can you marry, my poor darling? There is only one man in the world good enough for you, and he is mine. I cannot give him up, even to you, my saint. I have two saints now; I ought to be a Catholic. The second one is his mother, the Saint of Las Rosas, as she is called all through this part of the island. Marguerite, I must strive to grow like her, too, if such a thing were possible. I have work enough for my life, but what blessed work! to try to make myself worthy of Jack Delmonte, my Jack, my own!

He took me to his mother; I have just come from her. I am her daughter from that moment, she says; oh, Marguerite, I will try to be a good one. Hear me—no! I am not going to make vows any more, or talk like girls in novels; I am just going to try. I loved her from the first moment I saw her grave, beautiful face. She took me in her arms, my dear; she said things—I have come up here to weep alone, tears of happiness. Dearest, you alone knew thoroughly the old Rita, the foolish creature, who dies, in a way, to-night. Say good-bye to her; give her a kiss, Marguerite, for she too loved you; but not half as dearly as does the new, happy, blessed Margarita de San Real Montfort.

THE END